DIRTY HANDS
SCREENPLAY

**PUBLISHED BY
UNDERGROUND VOICES**
Copyright © 2017 Cetywa Powell
All rights reserved.
ISBN: 978-0990433187

CONTENTS

DIRTY HANDS

FADE IN ON:

1. EXT. STREET - NIGHT

A black screen. Sounds of congestion — cars, conversation, normality.

And then a CAR BOMB. SHATTERING GLASS. SENDING SHRAPNEL INTO NEARBY STRUCTURES, PEOPLE. LIGHTING UP THE SKY FOR A BRIEF MOMENT.

A HIGH-PITCHED SCREAM — A BOY'S. THEN CHAOS.

Shouts. Screams. Running feet against a pitch black night. A flashlight flickering on. Going over stunned faces.

And then a HUMVEE with 6 SOLDIERS in full combat gear coming down the street. Headlights beaming light on the burning car, on the bodies surrounding the wreckage.

COMBAT ARMED SOLDIERS EMERGING. GUNS POINTED AT THE FACES. FLASHLIGHTS ON WEAPONS FANNING THE AREA. A SMATTERING OF VOICES.
BLACKNESS.

A melodious voice.

                    MUEZZIN (V.O)
          A-l-l-a-a-h-u… A-a-k-b-a-r…

2. EXT. MOSQUE - DAY

Dawn. *Azan*. The call to prayer sounds out from a mosque's loudspeakers.

                    MUEZZIN (V.O)
          … Ash-hadu an la ilaha ill-
          Allah…

The voice carries over a seemingly tranquil land.

In the horizon, against a quiet backdrop, a blood-red sun signals another day.

3. INT. CAR - DAY

Suffocating heat. Rain. A moving car. Two SOLDIERS in desert tan uniforms and M-16 rifles in the front.

A MAN with a hood over his head in the back. Hands--handcuffed. A SOLDIER next to him. The car pulls up to a red light. Silence except for the windshield wipers creating brown streaks on the windshield, pushing away water, dust. Dirty rain.

The Soldier in the passenger seat lights a cigarette, smokes casually. Tobacco-stained fingers lift, motion to the left.

The car moves forward again, gliding smoothly, turning left. Destination unknown.

4. INT. HOTEL - MORNING

AN ARMY COMBAT UNIFORM ON A HOTEL ROOM BED: jacket, pants, t-shirt, combat boots. Hands move across the uniform, carefully removing select pieces. Snapping buttons. A wedding ring wrapped around the next to last finger.

Move up to LIEUTENANT COLONEL JOSEPH LEVINO in full army combat uniform. Strong physique. Tired eyes. A man not quite ready for battle.

Levino pulls the blinds open. Warm daylight pours in, the streets below alive with activity. He walks to the bathroom, past a DRIVING IRON against the wall.

5. EXT. STREET - LATER

A black SUV lurches down the trash-tossed road,
maneuvering around a car set on cinder blocks,
stripped to a battered frame.

6. INT./EXT. SUV - MOVING - SAME

Levino gazes silently out the window, face tense.
His eyes expand on--

7. EXT. STREET - SAME

DEAD BODIES, laying twisted and bullet-marked in
the street — smoke billowing over them.

Up ahead a detention building sits, shadowed
against the rising amber sun.

The Soldier, NELSON, in the driver's seat looks
through the rear-view mirror. Finds Levino's
eyes.

                    NELSON
          Welcome to the shithole sir.

Levino watches the filth lining the street, the
puddles of dirty water.

                    LEVINO
                  (quietly)
          Yeah.

He slumps back in his seat, closes his eyes.
Wishing to be anywhere but here.

                  TITLE CARD
      INTERMEDIATE DETENTION CENTER, UNDISCLOSED
                    LOCATION

8. INT. OFFICE - DAY

Daylight filters through the soot on the windows.

Levino stands in a corner of a dilapidated room, substituting for an office. He stops by one of the desks, runs his finger across the top of its surface. Pushing the grime away.

He walks to the window, looks out of the dirt-caked blinds, glancing down three flights, as FOUR HOODED DETAINEES are brought out of SUV's.

Levino's cell phone RINGS, startling him. COLONEL BILL LARSON'S VOICE on the other end.

> COLONEL LARSON (V.O)
> You're heading into a
> situation. One of your
> detainee's wife and
> child were just killed by
> insurgent fire.

Levino's eyes stay on the shackled detainees.

> COLONEL LARSON (V.O)
> (hesitates)
> Levino?

> LEVINO
> Yeah, I'm here.

The shackled Detainees are pushed into the abandoned building.

9. INT. DETENTION CENTER, BASEMENT - DAY

A basement. Bleak. A blast of light from a window set high in the wall. Otherwise, darkness. The room lets off an air of suspense, horror. The silence is deafening.

Inside, the four detainees: THREE MEN, ONE WOMAN. Hands handcuffed.

A heavy silence except for squeaking shoes across the basement's concrete floors.

HAMZA EL SAADAWI (16), standing, paces restlessly. Eyes wide, rimmed with fear. An aura of innocence about him. He kicks at the few cigarette butts on the floor, his feet making rhythmic clicks against the concrete floor.

SAMI ABDUL-AHAD (38) and LARBI BEN-HIDI (early 40's), sit against one of the walls.

Larbi raises his head, blood-shot eyes briefly opening. A silent man made more silent by captivity.

He gives Hamza a look. Hamza stops, uncomfortable.

AMIRA, Hamza's sister (26), looks to both men. Face calm, eyes fiery, black, determined.

Suddenly, in the distance, a sound. LOUD. JOLTING.

A BUZZ, THEN AN EXPLOSION, THEN ANOTHER LONG BUZZ.

A beat. THEN SEVERAL RANDOM EXPLOSIONS.

The room still. Hamza starts pacing, eyes jerking upwards, nervous.

Larbi meets Hamza's eyes, questioning.

                    HAMZA
          …They're listening to us.
          They're saying the first one's
          starting to crack.

Larbi's eyes close. His head falls back against the wall. Even with his eyes closed, he looks like a man who's seen too much.

                    LARBI
          Fine. Don't crack. Sit down.
          Shut up. Go to sleep. Do some
          thinking.

In the distance, HEAVY MACHINE-GUN FIRE.

                    SAMI
          How far is that?

                    LARBI
          A few kilometers maybe.

                    SAMI
          It's not their bullets…

                    LARBI
          No. It's a Kalashnikov.

They listen. The gunfire fades. Sami's face
clouds over.

Larbi keeps a calm gaze on Sami. Waits for eye-
contact.

Sami finally meets his eye.

                    LARBI
          …We were obeying orders…

                    SAMI
          Maybe.

Sami looks away.

                    SAMI
          But we're still going to die.

                    HAMZA
              (panicked, whispered)
          I was carrying out orders. I
          don't wanna die.

                    AMIRA
               (gently)
          Hamza.

Hamza stops, turns to Amira.

                    AMIRA
          Come here.

Hamza hesitates. He awkwardly goes over, sits
next to her.

Sami watches them.

Amira brings her handcuffed hands up, wipes sweat
off the side of his face. She runs her hand down
his coat, talks in his ear, calming him.

Hamza nods emphatically. Then he looks around the
room, tries to get up.

                    AMIRA
          Don't move.

                    HAMZA
          I have to move. If I stop, I
          think. I don't wanna think.

Amira pulls Hamza back down. He lets himself slip
down against her knees. She strokes his hair.

Hamza meets Sami's eyes then fearfully looks
away.
                    AMIRA
          Someone can help you…
               (pause)
          Khassem.

Larbi, quietly listening, suppresses a smirk.

Sudden footsteps in the hallway. Hamza pulls away from Amira abruptly. Sami comes to life. Haunted, sad eyes narrowing.

10. INT. HALLWAY OUTSIDE BASEMENT

A long, dungeon corridor. TWO SOLDIERS with M16s flank MAJOR ANDREW DELANEY, African-American Army Interrogator and Linguist.

They swiftly head towards the basement door.

Their combat boots ECHO in morbid cadence against the concrete floor.

11. INT. BASEMENT

The door opens. The Soldiers look in at them. They push the door open wider.

Delaney comes in with a Polaroid camera. He stands in front of Sami, crouches down. *Flash*. A picture.

The Polaroid camera spits out film.

Delaney moves to Larbi, waits for Larbi to sit up. Larbi doesn't budge. Delaney gives one of the Soldiers a look.

The Soldier comes over, suddenly pushes the butt of his gun into Larbi's head, points towards the camera.

A tense moment. The room looks on. Then Larbi slowly leans forward.

Flash.

Delaney moves towards Hamza and Amira. Two *flashes.* The Soldiers go out.

11. INT. DETENTION CENTER, SURVEILLANCE ROOM -
SAME

A bare room with three TV monitors and two
chairs. Levino and Delaney quietly watch the
detainees on the monitors.

                    DELANEY
               (points to Sami)
          He's the weak one.

Levino nods at the information, opens a bottle of
water, gulps it down. His eyes move from monitor
to monitor.

                    LEVINO
          Why wasn't the woman separated
          from the men?

                    DELANEY
          She requested to be near the
          kid.
               (points to Hamza)
          Said he was her brother.

Levino turns blood shot eyes on Delaney.
Hesitant.

                    DELANEY
          We're lettin' her have a little
          room right now.
             (Levino—still unconvinced)
          Better chance she'll cooperate.

Levino's stare flicks back to the monitors,
perturbed, not liking the setup.

                    LEVINO
          Which one's Larbi?

Delaney looks to the 3rd monitor.

                    DELANEY
          Him.

12. INT. APARTMENT - FLASHBACK

THREE MIDDLE EASTERN POLICEMEN — LIGHT BLUE
SHIRTS, BLACK PANTS, DARK SUNGLASSES — force open
a door leading into a small, cluttered room.
Inside, they stand above Larbi as he dresses.
Watching as his clothes go on: pants, then his
shirt.

They address him. Cordially.

                    POLICEMAN
          Sabah El Kheir.

They lead him out.

Behind them, A WOMAN, LARBI'S WIFE, wearing a
hijab with a BABY in her arms, watches from the
dining room. Wide-eyed. Quietly trembling.

13. INT. POLICE CAR - LATER

Larbi, hooded, sits in the back seat of a police
car. Besides him, a Policeman keeps a gun trained
on him.

14. INT. BATHROOM - DAY

A men's bathroom. Dirt and urine-stained walls.

Larbi, still blindfolded, is led in, handcuffed
to a pipe jutting out of the wall, next to a line
of urinals.

The Policeman removes the blindfold, leaves.
Larbi takes his surroundings in, watches the door
cautiously. Nothing.

LATER...

Larbi still at the urinal, snaps awake. Looks around him. His stare jerks to the sink, watches as water slowly drips from it. He eyes it desperately.

Then the door OPENS...

An OLDER MAN (50's)... charismatic, bald... comes in, smiling.

His name tag says GENERAL RAMONE LARRAINE but HE IS CLEARLY MIDDLE EASTERN. He stands over Larbi, eyes sharp, penetrating.

Larraine wraps a rubber object around his fist. Larbi stares, mesmerized.

                    LARRAIN
          Name?

                    LARBI
          Larbi.

Larraine suddenly slams his fist into Larbi's stomach. The rubber object sends an electrical shock through Larbi's body.

Larbi reels over, SCREAMING.

                    LARRAIN
                 (to himself)
          ...Larbi. That's the one.

Another fist SLAMS into Larbi. Larbi writhes from the jolt of electricity.

Larraine slugs Larbi in the stomach with a backhanded fist. Larbi slams back into the urinal.

Someone else steps forward — A SERGEANT. In his hand, a wooden CLUB. He swings it in the air, catches it in midair, then — THWACK

Smashes it right across Larbi's shins. Larbi SCREAMS.

The Sergeant walks the length of the bathroom, swinging his club. He goes to the window, listens.

O.S: a distant radio.

> RADIO (O.S)
> *...A new born King to see, pa rum pum pum pum... Our finest gifts we bring, pa rum pum pum pum... To lay before the king...*

The Sergeant smiles, looks down at Larbi. There's a strange silence. Then the Sergeant walks over.

> SERGEANT
> Think they're singin' for you?
> Think you're a poor little
> drummer boy?

The men in the room laugh. O.S: the Women keep going...

> RADIO (O.S)
> *I am a poor boy too, pa rum pum pum pum... rum pum pum pum... rum pum pum pum*

17. INT. BASEMENT

Larbi, silent.

> SAMI
> How did you get out?

                    LARBI
        They took me to the local
        police. I knew Ahmed. He let
        me go.

                    SAMI
        If it was me, I would've forced
        myself to hold out. Every
        minute, I would've said... hold
        out for another minute...
                (pause, looks to Larbi)
        Think that's a good method?

                    LARBI
        There are no methods.

Hamza shivers. His large, staring eyes go to the
floor.

                    LARBI
        Hamza.

Hamza doesn't react.

                    LARBI
                (more forcefully)
        Hamza.

Hamza looks up.

                    LARBI
        We do what we can to suffer as
        little as possible. The method
        doesn't matter.

Hamza visibly relaxes.

                    SAMI
        Doesn't make him any less of a
        coward.

                              LARBI
                      (turns on Sami)
                 What do you want? To know a
                 name, a date… so you can refuse
                 to talk? So you can show off
                 how brave you are?

Sami looks away. Larbi walks to the foot-long
window, looks out.

O.S: Music starts then stops.

A sudden silence. Then the music starts again.
Classical music. *Bach's Air in G String.*

The room listens, almost soothed by the majestic
violins soaring from above…

There's a silence. Calm. Therapeutic. The music
plays…

18. INT. DETENTION CENTER, HALLWAY – DAY

Levino and Delaney move towards the interrogation
room, carrying with them the intelligent analyst
package — detailed association matrixes,
interrogation highlights.

19. INT. DETENTION CENTER, STAIR WELL - SAME

CAPTAIN PHILLIP BAKER (36) average height,
stocky. Weathered eyes. His BDUS fitting him like
cardboard. He steps out from the dark stairway,
files in hand. Nervous. Trying to impress. He
salutes Levino.

                         BAKER
                 Colonel, I'm Captain Baker,
                 I'll be assisting in the
                 proceedings. Captain.

                    BAKER
          I hear you spent some time in
          the Utah National guard.

                    LEVINO
          Four years.

                    BAKER
          Marines too.

                    LEVINO
          They had me for eight years.

                    BAKER
                (tries a smile)
          ...Always hard on the wife.

                    LEVINO
          That's right Captain. Lookin'
          at a second divorce.

An awkward moment—Baker feeling a fool.

                    LEVINO
          What's the report say?

                    BAKER
          At Zero five oh five, three car
          bomb explosions at different
          locations in western Mosul: the
          Police Academy, the Al Wakas
          Police substation, and the Al
          Jamhori Hospital. At 10:10, a
          car bomb at the recruitment
          center. At 10:15, an attack
          north of the city.

                    LEVINO
          What are they claiming
          responsibility for?

                    BAKER
          ...We're holding them for the
          recruitment center bombing.

The interrogators go down a dark, ugly stairwell.

                    BAKER (cont'd)
          We suspect they also have a
          target list with names of key
          government officials. Plus
          there's possible involvement
          with the hostage. Brendan
          Widmark.

                    LEVINO
          Time crunch.

Baker nods.

The stairwell leads them to a corner doorway. A
malfunctioning light bulb flickers and BUZZES.

                    BAKER
          It says here you buckled under
          a time crunch.

Levino slows, pressing his stare on Baker.

                    LEVINO
          Are you reciting my file
          Captain or trying to get to
          know me?

Baker hesitates. Levino brushes past him,
entering the--

20. DETENTION CENTER, INTERROGATION ROOM

A wide room. Bare. A metal chair in the middle. A
table against one of the walls. A window on the
other end, overlooking ten stories. The men seat
themselves around the table.

O.S. Music. Loud. Distracting.

Baker lays out the Polaroid snapshots into a pyramid.

Delaney pulls out interrogation reports, summaries, a map from the packet.

                    DELANEY
          They're not Al Sadr's men and
          they're not foreign Islamist
          fighters.
                    (points to the map)
          Which leaves local insurgents
          operating in this area.

                    LEVINO
          Homegrown resistance. With
          possible foreign aid.

                    DELANEY
          Could be Shiites who have a
          stronghold here.

                    LEVINO
          Or Sunni fighters. More spread
          out. Different movements.
          Different tactics. Different
          goals.

Levino drops his look to the pyramid of Polaroids.

                    LEVINO
          Shiite or Sunni?

                    DELANEY
          Don't know.

O.S: the music pounds. Irritating.

                    LEVINO
         Baker. Tell the men to turn off
         that music.

                    BAKER
         We like to play it for--

                    LEVINO
         I don't care what you like,
         Captain.

                    BAKER
         Let's not start kicking each
         other's balls so early in the
         game.

Levino stops, looks up at Baker.

                    BAKER
         ...Sir.

Baker looses his smirk, heading out. Levino
rises, folding the map as he approaches the
window.

O.S The music stops. A sudden silence.

Levino faces the window, creating a sharp
silhouette.

                    LEVINO
              (points to the window)
         This is bad for interrogations.

                    DELANEY
         It's all we've got.

Levino turns around, takes in the rest of the
room, unimpressed.

A moment and Baker is back.

Levino silently studies the polaroids. He points
to Sami.

                    LEVINO
                  (to Baker)
         Get the first one.

Levino tears a piece of duct tape, covering his
name patch. He tosses the tape to Delaney, who
does the same.

21. INT. DETENTION CENTER HALLWAY - DAY

Flashlights streak darkness. Delaney and two
Soldiers move through a dark hallway, machine
guns slung over shoulders. They move towards the
basement.

22. INT. BASEMENT

The door opens.

                    SOLDIER
         Sami.

Pause. Sami slowly gets to his feet. Meets
Larbi's eyes. Larbi manages a reassuring smile.

The Soldiers lead Sami out.

23. INT. DETENTION CENTER HALLWAY

A U.S SOLDIER, SERGEANT LEVI SEDGWICK (23),
awkwardly places a white hood over Sami's head
then returns to position as Guard.

Two other Soldiers lead Sami forward, away from
the basement, down the hallway.

24. INT. BASEMENT

A long silence. Larbi swallows, closes his eyes.

A TV is suddenly BLASTED. Amira, Larbi, and Hamza exchange glances. The TV cuts off.

They all listen. Nothing except for drops of water from a crack in the ceiling.

Amira looks to Larbi. Larbi meets her eyes, holds the stare. They stay like this for a while. Eyes connected. Sharing the unknown.

Suddenly, O.S: Sami SCREAMS.

They all jump. Amira covers her ears. Sami's screams INTENSIFY.

Amira mumbles to herself, blocking out the sounds.

Then silence.

Amira takes her hands from her ears, looks back at Larbi. Larbi drops his eyes.

Hamza — visibly shaking — recoils into himself.

25. INT. DETENTION CENTER, OUTSIDE BASEMENT

Outside the basement door. Sedgwick stands guard. A moment of staring at a blank wall before SCREAMS crash him back into reality.

Anxious, Sedgwick pulls out a pair of headphones, turns on his *ipod*, slams the play button.

Music. Aerosmith. *Dream on.*

26. EXT. OUTSIDE THE DETENTION CENTER - EVENING

A black car pulls to a stop. A Soldier emerges from the passenger seat, goes to the back, opens the rear door.

He leads the hooded Man out, pushes him through the building's heavy steel door.

27. INT. DETENTION CENTER, ROOM - EVENING

A small room reserved for the FBI.

Two FBI AGENTS roll out the Man's fingerprints. The man gets slammed against a wall. The hood comes off.

Flash. A camera goes off, catching the Man off guard. Making him blink repeatedly. Then the hood returns, followed by the bright chrome leg and wrist irons…

28. INT. BASEMENT - LATER

The room — darker now. Suddenly, an overhead light flickers to life. Everyone looks up at the dim bulb hanging from the ceiling.

FOOTSTEPS in the hallway.

Larbi, eyes on the door. The door opens. Two Soldiers lead the hooded Man into the room.

The Soldiers go out, lock the door behind them.

The Hooded Man stands by the wall, then slowly sinks down to the floor.

A silence. Larbi, Amira, Hamza — watching.

The Hooded man brings his hands to his neck. He slowly lifts the sheet over his head.

A shocked silence.

KHASSEM (mid'30's, intelligent eyes) squints, eyes adjusting to the room, to everyone inside.

His eyes stop on Amira. A hint of pain, emotion. Amira's eyes flash disappointment.

                    KHASSEM
          I thought you were all dead.

The silence is long, tense.

                    LARBI
          How did you get caught?

                    KHASSEM
          A mistake. They raided the
          Ishtar hotel. Asked routine
          questions. I said I was a
          doorman there.

Larbi's eyes narrow.

                    KHASSEM (cont'd)
          I have the papers to prove it...

IN THE SURVEILLANCE ROOM

Delaney and a SOLDIER watch the monitor...

IN THE BASEMENT

Khassem takes in the room, the dejection. After a moment--

                    KHASSEM
          We can start again somewhere
          else.

                    LARBI
          You mean you can start again.

Khassem holds Larbi's stare.

NOISE O.S. The others look to the door, expectantly.

29. INT. HALLWAY - SAME TIME

Two Soldiers drag Sami, by the arms, down the
dungeon corridor.

30. INT. BASEMENT

The door opens. The Soldiers haul Sami in. Sami
collapses on the floor. The Soldiers leave.

A silence, heavy. Sami doesn't move.

                    HAMZA
          What did they do?

                    SAMI
                (quietly)
          Everything they could...

He slowly sits up.

                    SAMI
          They asked me where he was...
                (beat)
          If I knew, I would have said
          something...

The room — intensely silent. Sami looks up at
them, then follows their gaze into the dark
corner of the room.

He sees a shadow of a man. Larbi discretely
shakes his head.

                    LARBI
                (slowly, carefully)
          He's a doorman at the Ishtar
          hotel.

Sami looks away, pulls up against the wall. He
leans into it.

                    SAMI
              (shakes his head)
          Now I have something to hide.

                    LARBI
          We all have something to hide.

AN EXPLOSION IN THE DISTANCE. IT JARS THE ROOM.
Then a sudden silence.

                    SAMI
                  (quiet)
          It's wrong that one moment can
          destroy your whole life.

Sami scans the faces. Nervous energy gone. Eyes,
flatter, deader. His eyes fall on Larbi and stay
there.

                    SAMI
          If I had talked, would you be
          able to look me in the eye?

                    LARBI
          You wouldn't have talked.

                    SAMI
          But if I had?

Larbi says nothing.

31. EXT. ROOFTOP - INTERROGATION BUILDING - LATER

A golf ball is set upon a tee. A driving iron
SWOOPS by. CRACK. The golf ball soars across an
orange sunset. A pillar of smoke and fire burns
in the distance.

Levino stands with his driving iron. He pulls
another golf ball from his pocket, setting it on
the tee. He winds up, swings - CRACK! The ball
grows smaller against the sky.

EXPLOSIONS rumble across the landscape.

32. EXT. OUTSIDE DETENTION CENTER - NIGHT

CORPORAL TUCKER, (20) lights a cigarette, admiring the CLINK of his ZIPPO as he pockets it. The sweltering air steals his exhale. He wipes sweat beads off his wrinkled forehead, forcing a yawn.

Levino's boot heels KNOCK the ground. He approaches, CLAPPING his hands, swift and loud.

Tucker drops his cigarette, saluting. His eyes peeling open, bloodshot from lack of sleep.

>   LEVINO
>   Is there a problem Corporal?

>   CPL. TUCKER
>   Don't have enough security
>   personnel sir. We're stretched
>   thin.

Tucker goes for the front passenger door. Levino waves his hand.

>   LEVINO
>   I got it.

Tucker pauses, awkwardly. Then he goes to the driver's side.

33. INT. CAR - MOVING - NIGHT

They drive through mud. On the car's CD player, heavy metal pounds.

>   LEVINO
>   Can you turn that down?

Tucker awkwardly hits the off button. On his wrist, a tattoo: *"all gave some… some gave all."*

                    TUCKER
          Don't like this kind of music
          sir?

                    LEVINO
          Gives me road rage.

Tucker smiles.

In the distance, artillery lights up the sky,
streaking it with orange light. Somewhere else,
it could easily be fireworks.

                    TUCKER
          That shit's beautiful, Colonel.

Tucker swigs bottled water. He smiles as another
streak of orange lights up the sky.

                    LEVINO
          No it's not.

                    TUCKER
          Sure it is sir.

                    LEVINO
          That artillery's hittin'
          houses. Cars. People. It ain't
          beautiful at all.

                    TUCKER
          They're hitting us. We're
          hitting back sir.

                    LEVINO
          They're shootin' at us 'cuz
          they're scared. We're shootin'
          back 'cuz we're twice as
          scared.

                    TUCKER
          … I'm not scared Colonel.

                        LEVINO
          You should be.

Levino rolls his window down, feeling the night
desert air across his face.

                        TUCKER
                  (nervous, rambling on)
          I'm saying I never been afraid
          of buying it out here. I mean
          everyone's afraid of dying. And
          everyone's got a different way
          of dealing with it. I just keep
          thinking about the 11 meals I
          got left, the 5 more drives to
          my duty, the 3 more P.T.
          formations... maybe the 5 more
          times I gotta use the port-
          ajohn before I go home...

Levino looks away, uninterested.

Another FLASH, a slow-building RUMBLE. The two
men take in the passing desert.

From the surrounding mosques, suddenly the sound
of a call to prayer. Levino and Tucker exchange
looks.

                        TUCKER
          I see why people lose their
          mind in this place.

Levino gazes off in the distance, his mind
somewhere else.

                        LEVINO
                  (distracted)
          Used to be a peaceful sound.

                        TUCKER
          Captain Baker says Islam is
          what's wrong with this world.

LEVINO
Is that right?

Tucker looks at him, unsure how to respond.
The call to prayer dies out. Tucker rolls into
the BASE CAMP.

34. EXT. BASE CAMP - SAME

A stillness — quiet, peaceful. Levino using this
rare moment to watch Tucker's SUV disappear into
darkness.

And just as suddenly, the stillness is broken,
the quiet intervals of war gone … as GUNFIRE
erupts strong in the distance.

35. INT. HALLWAY - LATER

Down a narrow hallway. Levino, thoughtful,
absorbed. Passing Soldiers make a "hole" as he
walks through.

36. INT. BATHROOM - LATER

Levino's hand reaches to the sink to pick up a
razor. He carefully shaves, looking into a rust-
stained mirror, staring at the new creases lining
his eyes.

Outside, a poker game amongst the SOLDIERS.
LAUGHTER. CUSSING. SOLDIERS AT EASE.

Levino stops, something bothering him.

OUTSIDE

He emerges from his conex, approaches the
Soldiers. They all look to him, surprised. The
game stops, in midair. Levino scans the faces,
slowly, tired.

                         LEVINO
              Silence ladies.

An abrupt, respectful silence as the Soldiers
stare after him.

37. INT. LEVINO'S QUARTERS

Levino, facing a laptop. He hunches over it,
keying in his ID. A visual of JULIA (6)
comes up. She smiles into the web cam.

                         JULIA
              Hi daddy.

Levino's eyes glimmer.

                         LEVINO
              Hi pumpkin. Did you set this
              call up?

                         JULIA
                       (nodding)
              Huh huh.

                         LEVINO
              That's... very good.

Levino grinds his cigarette out, opens his desk
drawer, grabbing a book of children's stories.

                         LEVINO
              Which one?...

                         JULIA
              Princess Butterfly.

                         LEVINO
              Okay. What's my cell phone
              number?

Julia recites it with lightning speed.

                    JULIA
          415-335-2687

                    LEVINO
          Email address?

                    JULIA
          J-l-e-v-i-n-o at gmail.com

                    LEVINO
If you're in trouble?

                    JULIA
          Call your cell phone.
                    (a beat)
          ...And 911.

                    LEVINO
          Good.

Levino slowly sifts through pages, then looks up
at Julia, uncomfortable.

                    LEVINO
          Pumpkin?

Levino stops, suddenly vulnerable.

                    LEVINO
          ...Is Mom with another man?

                    JULIA
                    (hesitates)
          ...I think so.

Levino's eyes mask the sudden sting of this news.

                    LEVINO
          What's his name?

                    JULIA
          Umm... I forgot.

Levino finds Julia's request but he stares at the page for a few moments, ill at ease.

                    LEVINO
          ...Once upon a time there was a
          little butterfly that lived in
          the largest tree in the most
          magical forest and every night
          the butterfly would sit and
          watch as all the other butter-
          flies danced and sang under the
          light of a hundred lightning
          bugs...
                    (turns the page)
          ...and the butterfly just watched
          from far away, too shy to join
          the others...

Levino glances up at the screen. Julia smiles, lids heavy with sleep. Levino reaches up, gently touching her image.

38. LEVINO'S QUARTERS - LATER
Levino at the edge of his bed. On the phone. An edge to his voice.

                    LEVINO
          Are you alone?

On the other end, his wife, JANINE (44).

                    JANINE (V.O)
          Why?

                    LEVINO
          It's a simple question Janine.

                    JANINE (V.O)
          What's the real question Joe?

A beat. Uncomfortable.

                    LEVINO
Who's the man Julia told me
about?

                    JANINE (V.O)
Did she tell you or did you get
it out of her?

                    LEVINO
Who is he?

                    JANINE (V.O)
Joe. I'm single and I can see
anyone I damn well please.

                    LEVINO
You didn't answer the question.

CLICK.

Levino hits redial. This time, the answering
machine. He hangs up, rage in his eyes.

The phone rings. He grabs it. It's Baker.

                    BAKER (V.O)
Colonel… the men wanted me to
call you… to… they said…

                    LEVINO
Will you get to the goddamn
point.

A pause.

                    BAKER (V.O)
…We're back on, Colonel.

                    LEVINO
We need to eat first.

                    BAKER (V.O)
          Sir, while you eat, maybe I
          could get started with the
          questioning.

                    LEVINO
          No. You enjoy it too much.

Levino hangs up. Pulls his name tag off. Stares
into the darkness, deflated.

39. INT. HALLWAY, OUTSIDE INTERROGATION ROOM

Outside the Interrogation room, Levino about to
enter, suddenly decides against it. For the
moment. Instead he pulls out a cigarette, lights
it, slowly smokes. Savoring the quietness and
stillness of the hallway.

40. INT. INTERROGATION ROOM - LATER
The room: hot, airless. Heavy metal music pulses
from the radio.

An arm drops in, flips the radio off, pours
bottled water into a paper cup. It's Levino. He
turns, facing Baker and Delaney.

Baker, moody, sits with his arms folded.

                    LEVINO
          Something on your mind,
          Captain?

Levino's tone makes the room uncomfortable.

                    BAKER
          Yeah.
                    (defiant)
          We're not breaking 'em sir.

                    LEVINO
          You think you know how to break
          'em?

                    BAKER
        Sure. Sleep deprivation. If
        they pass out, I will
        personally be there to wake
        them the fuck up.
                (wound up, tight)
        I got Nelson's notes. I know
        who's been crying. Who's
        scared. Who's gonna talk.

                    LEVINO
        Baker, I understand you've been
        sharing your personal views
        with the lower ranks.

Baker almost laughs out loud, catching himself.
The disrespect is growing more evident to Levino.

                    LEVINO
        Let me make something clear to
        both of you men before we go on.
        We don't conduct proceedings with
        any disregard for the fact that
        those are human beings. And when
        they're in this room we are going
        to treat them as such. And we're
        sure as hell not going to force
        any violence or personal hatred
        into this situation. Understand?

                DELANEY/BAKER
        Yes sir.

                    LEVINO
        Baker, go see if the food's
        here.

Baker paces, not pleased.

                    BAKER
        Just me and them alone,
        Colonel. I'll get you anything
        you want.

                      39

                    LEVINO
          Captain. Food. Go. Now. And get
          someone to clean this up.

Baker stops at the door.

                    LEVINO
          Why are you still here?

                    BAKER
          I don't think we should clean
          it up sir.

                    LEVINO
          We got to eat here, dammit.

Levino grinds his cigarette out on the table.

                    BAKER
          With all due respect sir, we
          shouldn't clean it up.

                    LEVINO
          We're not leaving another man's
          blood on the floor for show.

Baker stands a moment, pissed. He leaves finally.

In the distance, an Apache helicopter. Loud at
first then it fades away, into a soft drone.

                    DELANEY
                    (quiet)
          I hate it here.

                    LEVINO
          You're gonna hate it more.
          We're looking at two bombs a
          day. A growing insurgency.
          Situation's about to boil over.

Delaney, quiet. He goes back to the window,
stares out. An almost handsome face.

                    DELANEY
          I plan on putting in for early
          leave…

                    LEVINO
          You can't. Place is too
          unstable. This will be your
          life for another year Major.
          Start enjoying it.

Delaney's expression shifts. There's something
sad in his stare…

                    DELANEY
          At least one of us is comfortable
          here.

                    LEVINO
          Not comfortable. Dedicated.

                    DELANEY
          Never wanted a normal-style
          life?

                    LEVINO
          Never been good at it.

Delaney takes off his glasses, methodically wipes
them.

                    DELANEY
          Normality's good. Keeps me
          sane.

In the distance, a cluster bomb. The noise jars
Delaney back to reality.

                    DELANEY
          Baker may be good at this fear
          up approach but he'll get us
          court martialed.

                    LEVINO
          Word is we're doing a fine job.

                    DELANEY
                  (bitter laugh)
          Fine job? No, I wouldn't call
          it that.

Levino gives Delaney a look, says nothing.

                    DELANEY
                   (distant)
          One of them asked me my name. I
          almost told him.

                    LEVINO
          Don't get an attack of morality
          just 'cuz you look like them.

Delaney turns.

                    DELANEY
                    (icy)
          Sorry?

                    LEVINO
          Don't be a detainee lover.

                    DELANEY
          What the fuck does that mean?

The door opens. SSG Sedgwick comes in,
interrupting.

                    LEVINO
                (to Sedgwick)
          Get a non rate to clean up that
          mess.

Levino points to the blood staining the floor and
wall.

Sedgwick nervously double-glances the blood, heading out.

Levino eyes Delaney coolly.

> LEVINO
> I run these interrogations
> Major. Like I told the Captain,
> I don't need personal feelings
> gettin' in the way.

Delaney glares, swallowing anger.

Baker returns carrying three trays. He WHISTLES, laying out the trays and silverware.

> BAKER
> If we really want to shake up
> the detainees we can feed them
> some of this slop.

The door opens again. A SOLDIER shuffles through with a mop and bucket. He stands over the blood, holding back his discomfort.

Finished, he stands, waits for orders. Levino catches his eye.

> LEVINO
> (to Soldier)
> Give us another ten minutes.

The Soldier nods, goes out. Baker resumes humming. Levino picks up his fork. The others follow suit…

> LEVINO
> We're running out of time.

                    BAKER
          How much do you expect to get
          out of 'em when we got 'em set
          up at a day camp sir? I got
          Nelson's notes. I know who's
          been crying. Who's scared...

                    LEVINO
          You said that already.

Baker smolders. Levino turns to Delaney.

                    LEVINO
          The senior guy. Larbi. What's
          he like?

                    DELANEY
          Proud. Tough.

                    BAKER
          You mean he's a piece of shit.

Delaney slides his tray away, fed up. He stands,
heading to the window. Baker scoops food off
Delaney's tray, eats messily. Levino shoots him a
look, irritated.

Delaney pushes the window open. Outside, the
distant POPPING of MACHINE GUN FIRE.

                    BAKER
          Don't open the window. Dust
          will get in the food.

Delaney starts to close the window.

                    LEVINO
          No, leave it open.

Baker meets Levino's eyes, drops them, face
twisting with anger.

The Soldier, Nelson, comes in. All men look to
him.

> NELSON
> Widmark got beheaded. It aired
> at twenty two hundred hours.
> Local TV.

Levino drops his stare. Baker crosses his arms.
Delaney shuts his eyes.

> LEVINO
> Did they get a copy of it?

> NELSON
> Yes sir.

> LEVINO
> Bring it in.

41. A LAPTOP

BRENDAN WIDMARK, 52. Orange jumpsuit. Facing the
camera,a rifle pointed to his head.

> WIDMARK
> ...My name is Brendan Widmark.
> I'm a British National and I
> have worked with American
> forces...

Widmark's hands wring non-stop.

> WIDMARK
> ...I have been arrested by a
> resistance group. I am asking
> for help because... my life is in
> danger... because it's been
> proved that I worked for
> American forces...

The tape goes black. Static. Then a Voice spits
out harsh, angry Arabic.

Another image on-screen. Widmark faces the camera, seated on the floor, wearing a white blindfold and an orange jumpsuit. Arms bound behind his back.

Behind him, FIVE BLACK-CLAD MEN, armed with AK-47's, wear black ski masks over their faces.

The accusatory sounds are from the EXECUTIONER in the middle, as he reads from a white piece of paper. His speech — clipped, hurried, emphatic.

> EXECUTIONER
> *(classical Arabic)*
> Allahu Akhbar. We have beheaded the second American hostage after the expiration of the deadline. We will execute the British hostage since the British government has not pulled out... We will take revenge for the blood of our brothers...

The Executioner leans down to Widmark. Pulls a knife from his belt. Saws at Widmark's throat. Widmark SCREAMS.

42. INT. BASEMENT - LATER

FOOTSTEPS outside. Everyone in the basement looks towards the door. The door opens.

Two SOLDIERS with M-16's stand behind Sergeant 1st Class Nelson. Nelson points to Larbi. Larbi slowly rises, goes out.

The room quietly watches him go.

43. INT. INTERROGATION ROOM - DAY

Larbi is led into the room with Delaney, Baker, and Levino. Levino measures him.

                    LEVINO
                   (calm)
         Put him in that chair. Take his
         hood off. Handcuff his wrists
         to the chair.

The Soldiers lead him into a chair, handcuff him
down.

The hood comes off Larbi's head. His head jerks
down, eyes reacting to the light. Bloodshot eyes
take the room in.

A MIDDLE EASTERN POLICEMAN, TALAT, standing on
the side — black pants, blue shirt, a bulletproof
vest with the words POLICE in yellow Arabic
across the front — watches Larbi.

                    LEVINO
         What sect are you from?

Delaney repeats the question in Arabic.

                    DELANEY
                 (classical Arabic)
         Tribe?

A long beat before Larbi answers.

                    LARBI
         Sunni.

                    LEVINO
         How many in your Jihad?

                    DELANEY
                 (in Classical Arabic)
         How many fighting for Jihad?

                    LARBI
                 (in Arabic)
         Muqawima not Jihad.

All eyes go to Delaney.

                    DELANEY
          They're resistance fighters,
          fighting for their country. Not
          religious fighters.

Larbi nods. Levino looks to him.

                    LEVINO
              (to Delaney)
          He understands what I'm saying.

                    DELANEY
          (*to Larbi, in Classical Arabic*)
          Do you speak English?

Larbi lifts his head. Meets Levino's eyes.

                    LARBI
          Yes.

                    LEVINO
          Good.

Levino steps forward.

                    LEVINO (cont'd)
          You smoke?

Larbi nods. Levino pulls out a cigarette from a
packet in his pocket, lights it, sticks it in
Larbi's mouth. Larbi inhales once, keeps the
cigarette on the corner of his mouth.

                    LEVINO
          How old are you?

                    LARBI
          ...It's in the file.

                    LEVINO
                 (to Larbi)
        I'd like to hear it from you.

No answer.

                    DELANEY
        Your wife wants you home. We
        talked to her this morning.
        We'd like to help her. But in
        order to do that, we need your
        help.

Levino drops his eyes. A flicker of emotion,
hesitation, then it's gone. He looks back up at
Larbi.

                    LEVINO
        Look at us Larbi. We're the
        only people who can help you.
                 (pauses)
        The boy, Hamza, told us he
        distributed the guns for your
        group.

Larbi's head snaps up.

                    LARBI
        When?

                    LEVINO
        When the FBI took his prints.
                 (beat)
        He also said you're not the
        leader...

Larbi's eyes narrow.

                    LEVINO
        ...but you still know where the
        target list is.

Silence.

                    LEVINO (cont'd)
          The hostage on your list just
          got beheaded. Who's the next
          name on that list?

Larbi looks away.

                    LEVINO
          It's better for you to admit
          everything.

                    LARBI
          Admit what?

                    LEVINO
          Give us the names of all the
          people on that list.

                    LARBI
          What people?

Levino yanks the cigarette out of Larbi's mouth,
stubs it out.

                    LEVINO
          I've been doing this for ten
          years Larbi and I'm damn good
          at my job. So think real hard
          about what you're doing because
          I will win this one.

A beat. Nothing from Larbi.

                    LEVINO (cont'd)
          Alright Baker.

Baker looks to Talat, the policeman in the room.
Nods. Talat hoods Larbi. Drags him out.

44. INT. SMALLER ROOM - SAME TIME

In another room, loud music — *David Gray's
Babylon* — suddenly cuts off.

Eight SOLDIERS watch as Larbi is led into the room.

Larbi is positioned on a FOOD BOX.

> SOLDIER
> (to Abu Talat)
> Keep his hands lifted. Clip the electrical cords between his fingers.

Abu Talat clips the cords between Larbi's fingers.

An ELECTRICAL CURRENT SHOOTS THROUGH LARBI. Larbi SCREAMS, falls off the FOOD BOX.

A SOLDIER approaches. Kicks Larbi in the gut.

> SOLDIER
> Get up.

Larbi awkwardly and painfully gets up.
A second ELECTRICAL CURRENT. Larbi collapses on the floor.

The same Soldier steps forward. Another kick to Larbi's gut.

> SOLDIER (cont'd)
> Get up!

Larbi stays on the floor.

> SOLDIER
> Get up!

The Soldier nods towards Talat. A THIRD ELECTRICAL CURRENT.

A second Soldier steps forward, puts headphones from an *ipod* underneath the hood, into Larbi's ears.

The Soldier slowly MAXES THE VOLUME. HITS PLAY. DAVID GRAY'S BABYLON SLAMS INTO LARBI'S EARS.

45. OUTSIDE THE INTERROGATION ROOM, HALLWAY

Baker paces, taking hits off a cigarette.

46. INT. INTERROGATION ROOM

>   DELANEY
>   You need to rein the Captain
>   in.

Levino ignores him, looks through Larbi's file.

>   LEVINO
>   I need him to talk.

>   DELANEY
>   Sure. But good results don't
>   justify bad acts.

A beat.

>   LEVINO
>   You're getting soft Delaney.

Delaney ignores him. Levino looks up.

>   LEVINO (cont'd)
>   I wondered about some of these
>   guys when I started this. How
>   we treated them. Now I don't
>   care. It's a job. I want it
>   done. And I wanna go home.

Baker comes into the room, sticks a pack of cigarettes in his pocket.

                    LEVINO
                 (to Baker)
        Baker, I don't need them dead.
        I need their target list. Don't
        get us court-martialed.

                    BAKER
        This'll get us answers.

                    LEVINO
        No it'll get us fired. Get him
        back in here.

                    BAKER
        He could use a little more
        softening up.

                    LEVINO
        Get him back in here.

                    BAKER
        If we're harder…

                    LEVINO
        You have a problem with that
        order Captain?

The two men lock eyes. Masked hatred in both.
Baker looks away first. Leaves.

47. INT. INTERROGATION ROOM - LATER

Levino drums his fingernails on the table.
Anxious.

He checks his watch. Eyes the door.

                    LEVINO
        Where the fuck is he?

48. INT. DETENTION CENTER, SURVEILLANCE ROOM

Levino pushes the door open, glancing at the
monitors.

                    LEVINO
          Where's Larbi?

                    SEDGWICK
          Sir, Captain Baker is prepping
          the prisoner.

Levino turns, annoyed as he heads out.

49. INT. HALLWAY - SAME

Levino picks up his pace, moving down the
hallway.

50. INT. DETENTION CENTER, ROOM - SAME

Levino throws the door open. Baker, Nelson, and a
SOLDIER stand over Larbi.

Larbi's on a flat surface, a cloth over his head,
the Soldier pouring water over him.
Waterboarding.

The room stops. The water stops. A heavy silence.
Levino steps up to Larbi, pulls the cloth off,
uncuffs his hands. Levino ushers Larbi out of the
seat.

                    LEVINO
               (to the soldier)
          Get him cleaned up.

Levino helps Larbi out the door.

51. HALLWAY

Delaney and the Policeman, Talat, sit on a bench outside the interrogation room. Talat loosens his bullet-proof vest.

Baker comes down the hallway, lighting a cigarette. For the first time, Baker looks exhausted. He takes a hit, tired eyes taking a good look at Delaney.

> BAKER
> You think I enjoy this but I
> don't.

Delaney looks unconvinced.

> BAKER (cont'd)
> Those Arabs killed their own.
> I've never killed anyone.

A long silence.

Baker stubs out his cigarette, goes back into the room.

Delaney, stoic, stares at the wall. Then he follows Baker inside.

Talat, alone, takes deep breaths. Pained eyes staring off into the distance. Quiet. Still. He's learned to hold it in.

52. INT. BASEMENT - NIGHT

In the stillness — without gunfire, without the overhead apache helicopter, without the cluster bombs — Khassem, Sami, Amira, and Hamza kneel on white place mats, facing Mecca.

They quietly pray.

53. INT. BASEMENT - NIGHT

Sedgwick's eye looks through the peep-hole
leading into the basement. He steps in, eyeing
the room cautiously.

Then he steps in front of Sami, pulls out a pack
of cigarettes, extends one towards him. Sami
takes it, eyes carefully rising to meet
Sedgwick's.

Sedgwick looks around. Amira and Hamza shake
their heads.

The Soldier turns to Khassem. Khassem nods.
Sedgwick moves over to him, hands him a
cigarette, lights it. Their eyes meet. They hold
the stare. Two men. Separate worlds. Somehow… an
understanding. Slight.

The match goes out. Sedgwick looks at the faces
then quietly and awkwardly leaves.

54. EXT. ROOFTOP - DAY

A golf ball sits on a tee. Gunfire POPS in the
distance. The driver comes down. WHACK! The ball
is gone. Levino sets another golf ball on the
tee.

Delaney comes up behind Levino. Watches him for a
moment.

                    DELANEY
          So you're just going to let him
          find out on his own?

Levino lines up his shot.

                    LEVINO
          A man finds out he's just lost
          his family. He's got nothing.
          Why should he cooperate?

56

                    DELANEY
        Because he doesn't have much of
        a choice, and we need to
        reinforce that. We can't afford
        to come up empty on this.

Levino swings, launching another golf ball into
the sky.

55. INT. DETENTION CENTER, TV ROOM

Levino sits, facing a TV, with his lap-top opened
to Larbi's file. The table in front of him,
covered with Larbi's documents: photos,
photocopied licenses, reports…

Larbi holds up a photo of Larbi posing with a
DIPLOMA. Levino looks through more documents: a
hand-scrawled note, a photocopy of Larbi's
driver's license, documents from Larbi's job.

He clicks open a jpeg image: a recent picture of
Larbi with his wife.

The picture gives Levino pause and he stares at
it for a while — the haunting sad image of a man
who could be any man, anywhere.

SEVERAL RANDOM EXPLOSIONS SHAKE THE BUILDING.

Levino looks to the window, jolted from this
thoughts. The laptop image shudders…

56. INT. AMIRA'S HOUSE, LIVINGROOM – FLASHBACK

*The outskirts of Baghdad. Second hand furnishing:
an old T.V on a wooden stand, Amira's family
photos on top of a small table stand, other
framed pictures of a past life. A happier life.*

*On one side of the living room, Khassem with his
PARENTS.*

On the other side, Amira on a wooden chair.

Next to her: Hamza and few immediate relatives…
AUNTS AND UNCLES, two older LADIES. Here to
celebrate Amira's engagement to Khassem.

Amira wears a long modest dress with a white
scarf wrapped over her head. Khassem, a double
breasted suit.

THE MOMENT OF TRUTH

Khassem's mother hands him 10 bracelets of 22
carats gold, wrapped in white silk cloth. Khassem
rises, goes to Amira, goes down on one knee,
unwraps the cloth, places five sets of bracelets
on each hand.

After the last bracelet, the room erupts in
cheers. The Women — smiling, laughing — break
out, in unison, with the HALHOLA.

57. INT. BASEMENT

Khassem smokes silently, facing Amira, eyes
showing concern, deep love.

Amira meets his stare, sees the worry.

                    AMIRA
                (gently)
        I won't scream.

                    KHASSEM
        Hamza will scream.

                    HAMZA
        You're right. I'm not a hero. I
        refuse to be martyred for you.

Sami shoots Hamza a look then slowly shakes his
head.

Khassem says nothing, gaze calm. Steady.

Sami pulls hard on his cigarette, scrutinizing
Khassem. He exhales a cloud of smoke.

> SAMI
> (to Khassem)
> I'm glad you're here. First,
> because you see things
> differently…
> (smiles)
> Second, because you'll be a
> witness. Dying with no
> witnesses is a real waste.

Both laugh. Morbidly. Sami suddenly turns
serious.

> SAMI (cont'd)
> When you get out, go see my
> father and write to Larbi's
> wife. Tell them about this.

> KHASSEM
> Where's your father?

> SAMI
> He should be where I left him,
> inshallah. He's a landowner.
> On Amrim street, in Dhuluaya.

Sami turns to Amira.

> SAMI
> What about you Amira?

No response. Khassem looks to Hamza. Hamza keeps
his head down.

> SAMI (cont'd)
> Amira?

                    AMIRA
                  (quietly)
        There's no one. My father
        forged a passport and left the
        country when I was five and
        Hamza was one.
                    (a beat)
        I missed a whole school year
        waiting for him to send for us.
        He never did.

Hamza looks at Amira.

                    AMIRA
        My mother died a few years
        later. So there's no-one.

Amira lifts her head. There is intense feeling in
her eyes.

Khassem takes a step towards her. FOOTSTEPS
outside stop him. Sami motions Khassem back into
the corner.

Khassem hesitates, holds Amira's stare then backs
into the corner.

The door opens. Larbi appears, badly beaten,
flanked by Soldiers. The door shuts.

Silence. The room absorbs Larbi.

59. INT. INTERROGATION ROOM - DAY

The TV on: an interview in progress. The MAN
being interviewed sits cross-legged, a pillow on
his lap. 40's. Short, graying hair.

He occupies a bare room, with one fluorescent
light. A tattered white curtain hangs over the
single window.

                    INSURGENT
          ...I joined the ranks of the
          insurgents after 30 men I knew
          died...

The Insurgent's 3-year old son plays next to him,
shining a flashlight in his father's eyes.

                    INSURGENT
          ...I have carried out 17 or 18
          operations and when I shoot a
          target with a rocket-propelled
          grenade, it's like celebrating
          a feast...

The Insurgent's voice drops. He shakes his head.

                    INSURGENT (cont'd)
          ...but I swear by the holy Koran
          that no one is beheaded unless
          he confesses that he did
          something to help the...

Click. The TV goes off. Levino turns to the
others.

Frustration, all consuming.

                    LEVINO
          We're losin' time.

Baker picks at left-over food. Delaney, silent,
watches both of them.

                    LEVINO
          Get the girl.

                    BAKER
          I don't think we can break her
          fast enough sir.

Baker looks up at the pyramid layout of the
Polaroids. Amira and Hamza are at the bottom.

                    BAKER (cont'd)
              The first one's ready.
                 (points to Sami's Polaroid)
              He's gonna talk.

Levino looks to Delaney. Delaney nods.

                    LEVINO
              Alright.

Baker goes out.

                    DELANEY
              They're martyrs. They're gonna
              be difficult.

                    LEVINO
              Amateur martyrs.

Delaney looks to Levino.

                    LEVINO (cont'd)
              Resistance fighters with no
              outside help.

A blank stare from Delaney.

                    LEVINO
              Means we can break 'em.

Levino stands in front of the Polaroids. There's
something concentrated in his stare. Calmer.

60. INT. BASEMENT

Two Soldiers fling the door open.

                    SOLDIER
              Sami.

Sami stiffens, eyes panic-stricken.

                              SAMI
           Oh no. No…

He looks to Larbi. This time Larbi keeps his eyes
down.

Sami doesn't move. He just hangs his head,
shaking it back and forth…

                         SAMI (cont'd)
              No, no, no…

The Soldiers walk up to him, grab him by his
shirt, yank him to his feet. Sami's voice,
increasing in volume. Screaming now.

                              SAMI
              NO! NO! NO! NO!

The Soldiers haul him out. The door slams. Sami's
cries can be still be heard…

61. INT. INTERROGATION ROOM

The two Soldiers bring Sami in. Sami looks like a
man who's just lost it.

                             BAKER
                      (to the Soldiers)
              Handcuff his arms to the chair.

The Soldiers do as instructed then go out.

62. HALLWAY

Outside the door, the Soldiers exchange a LOOK.
Fear. Hesitation. *What the fuck?!*

A beat. They walk away from the door.

63. INTERROGATION ROOM

Baker goes to Sami, looks into his eyes,
suspending the moment. Then Baker goes to the
table, pours a glass of whiskey. He takes it to
Sami.

> BAKER
> Drink.

Sami turns his head away. Baker yanks Sami's head
forward, force-feeds him the whiskey.
Sami gags, spits it out.

> BAKER
> When I tell you to drink you
> fuckin' whore, you drink.

More whiskey. Down Sami's throat. Sami retches,
vomits this time.

> BAKER
> You know why you're back?

> DELANEY
> (in classical Arabic)
> Do you know why you're here?

Sami swallows. He shakes his head.

> BAKER (cont'd)
> Because you're a coward and
> you're gonna squeal. Like a
> fuckin' pig. Like the shit you
> won't eat. You a coward?

Sami doesn't answer.

> DELANEY
> (in Classical Arabic)
> Sami. You have the power to
> make this stop.

No reaction. Sami's eyes are blank, fixed on a point in space, watching something, an imaginary movie.

                    BAKER
                 (to Talat)
          Take his handcuffs off.

Talat carefully removes Sami's handcuffs.

                    BAKER
          Get up.
Sami nervously stands. Swaying. Delaney looks away.

SUDDENLY BAKER GRABS SAMI AND HAULS HIM TOWARDS THE WINDOW, FORCING HIM HALF-WAY OUT.

Sami SCREAMS from fear, shock.

                    BAKER
          Feel like talkin' now, you dumb
          fuck?

                    LEVINO
          That's enough.

Baker shoves Sami further out the window.

                    LEVINO
                 (harder)
          THAT'S ENOUGH.

Baker turns to Levino, about to protest.

SUDDENLY SAMI JUMPS ON THE WINDOWSILL. There's an amazing agility to his movements… the last of his strength.

The room freezes.

Sami stands between life and death, his eyes shining with tears.

                         SAMI
                  (softly, in Arabic)
          I won.

Talat takes a step forward, stretches his arm out
in front of him to calm Sami. For the first time,
Talat speaks.

                     ABU TALAT
                    (in Arabic)
            No Sami.
Sami briefly looks into Talat's eyes, holding the
window to keep steady. His eyes dart across the
room in wild desperation. He leans back, towards
open air.

SUDDENLY HE SHOUTS.

                         SAMI
              SAMAANA-WA-ATAANA!

Abut Talat rush towards him. Sami sees him
coming, JUMPS FROM THE WINDOW.

A collective GASP.

Abu Talat closes his eyes. A shocked silence as
the Interrogators look at the vacant spot.

                       LEVINO
            Fuck! Fuck, fuck, fuck!

Levino goes to the window, looks down ten
stories.

                       LEVINO
                     (to Talat)
            Go down after him.

Talat goes out.

                    BAKER
                (to Delaney)
    I told you to close the window.

Levino goes up to Baker, SLAPS him hard.

                    LEVINO
        Put that in your report.

Baker, startled, steps back from Levino. Sits in
Sami's chair.

A tense silence as the men wait. Finally, Talat
comes back.

                    TALAT
        He's dead.

Pause. The three men look at each other.

                    LEVINO
        Get the girl.

64. INT. HALLWAY - DAY

Another shift. A different SOLDIER stands guard
outside the closed basement door. Two others drag
Amira down the hallway.

65. INT. BASEMENT - EVENING

A cold, dead silence. Everyone sits apart, in
their own world. There's something different
about the room, something resigned.

Larbi speaks, to no-one in particular.

                    LARBI
            They hung me upside down, about
            30 centimetres from the floor.
            And they kept shocking me...
            sporadically...

A long stretch of silence. Khassem turns, eyes slowly focusing, as though from a long stupor.

> LARBI
> And all I could think about was a song… over and over… this Abba song… and I said… I can't die with that song going through my head. That stupid Abba song. That's all I thought about…

A beat.

> KHASSEM
> Which one?

> LARBI
> …Take a chance on me.

They meet eyes. Khassem tries to suppress a smile.

> KHASSEM
> (quietly)
> *If you change your mind, I'm the first in line…*

> LARBI
> *…I'm still free… Take a chance on me…*

They both laugh. Larbi rubs his swollen wrists.

> KHASSEM
> No handcuffs.

Larbi shakes his head.

Hamza jerks his head up, puzzled by Larbi's two free hands. He hadn't noticed it. Hamza looks away.

Faint footsteps outside. This time no one reacts.
The footsteps recede into silence.

> KHASSEM
> Look at us. Resisting the
> occupiers. But in the end, what
> good will it do?

> LARBI
> What do you mean?

> KHASSEM
> I was in *AlShoarjah*. You know
> how the traffic jams are. One
> of the drivers went up on the
> sidewalk to avoid the traffic.
> And I walked past the car and
> said, 'What are you doing,
> driving here? You can't just
> drive anywhere you want.' And
> he said, 'Of course I can. It's
> the new freedom. I can do
> whatever I want.'

Suddenly — O.S: an EXPLOSION. All three look
towards the window.

> KHASSEM
> I used to read about how the
> Lebanese got used to the bombs
> in Beirut. I never thought that
> would happen to me.

Larbi says nothing. Khassem keeps his eyes on the
window, trying to measure time.

> KHASSEM
> I never told Amira I loved her.

Larbi looks away. After a while. Quietly.

> LARBI
> It doesn't matter.

The sound of GUNFIRE. Khassem's stare goes back
to the window.

                    KHASSEM
          …It's been two hours.

                    LARBI
          They enjoy themselves with
          women.

The implication hits Khassem hard. Hurts him.

                    KHASSEM
                    (angry)
          We'll attack. Sporadically.
          Break their will.

Larbi — quiet. He stares straight at Khassem.

                    LARBI
          Why did they bring you here?

                    KHASSEM
          Who?

                    LARBI
          The Soldiers.

                    KHASSEM
          What do you mean?

                    LARBI
                    (slow)
          Why did they bring you here
          with us?

A cautious beat.

                    KHASSEM
          I don't know.

                    LARBI
          You don't know?

Khassem holds the stare, bothered. Then he turns away, uneasily, looks around the room. His eyes shift to Hamza. He walks underneath the window, motions to Hamza to help him up.

Khassem climbs on Hamza's shoulders, looks out the window. His expression pales.

Khassem jumps to the floor.

> HAMZA
> I want to see.

Khassem helps Hamza up. Larbi's eyes follow Hamza with concern.

> LARBI
> You shouldn't.

Hamza ignores Larbi, looks out the 12-inch long window. His face shows the shock of what he sees. He climbs down, crouches in the corner, trembling.

Larbi shoots Khassem a hard look. Hamza stays bent over, about to vomit.

> HAMZA
> They found Abdul Jassim's body
> on the street like that. Then
> the soldiers tried to pay his
> family off…

> LARBI
> (hard)
> Don't worry about Sami. He's
> finished. Worry about yourself.

Khassem sits across from Larbi. Larbi stares at him hard, a measure of respect lost.

> KHASSEM
> I didn't force him.

66. INT. OFFICE

An office. Military decorations on the wall, the desk. Otherwise the office looks barely lived in. COLONEL BILL LARSON, U.S. ARMY INTERROGATOR (56) watches the news, ill at ease.

> REPORTER (V.O)
> *…The militants threatened to kill the US civilian hostage captured yesterday unless the siege of the mosque ended. Emil Curling, who was captured by gunmen on Friday, identified himself to a reporter. The kidnapping follows the recent beheading of British hostage Brendan Widmark…*

Colonel Larson dials a number, eyes riveted to the TV screen.

> COLONEL BILL LARSON
> (into phone)
> Washington's going to be coming down on us like God's wrath itself after what happened over there…

67. INT. DETENTION CENTER, HALLWAY

Levino, on the phone, moving down the hallway.

> COLONEL BILL LARSON (V.O)
> Your prisoner's suicide is gonna bring an investigation.

> LEVINO
> The circumstances were…

> COLONEL BILL LARSON (V.O)
> (cutting him off)
> Did you tell the detainee about
> his wife and kid?

> LEVINO
> Not yet.

> COLONEL BILL LARSON (V.O)
> Well goddamnit Levino, do your
> job!

The phone goes dead. Levino shuts his phone, eyes saying it all. *Shit.*

68. EXT. STREET - LATER

A KIOSK selling lunch. Busy. Cramped. Civilians and Soldiers crowd the stand. Talat, in line, waits his turn.

Levino stands apart from the crowd, waits for Talat's eye contact. When Talat sees him, Levino turns, walks away.

Talat follows.

69. INT. HALLWAY, OUTSIDE BASEMENT - LATER

Levino walks with Talat. They reach the basement door. Levino hangs back as Talat opens the door, heading in.

NEW ANGLE - LEVINO'S POV

Through the cracked door, Larbi sits bathed in soft daylight glowing in the window above.

Talat's shadow falls over Larbi's face. Talat leans in, speaking quietly to Larbi.

RESUME - LEVINO

As he turns away, heading off down the darkened
hall.

70. INT. LEVINO'S OFFICE

An image of a woman, JANINE, comes on screen.
Sad, distant, eyes red-rimmed.

A moment as she looks candidly at Levino. She
turns away finally.

                    JANINE
          …Here's Julia.

And then Julia is on the screen. Eyes wide-eyed,
questioning.

                    JULIA
          Is it true you're not gonna
          live with us anymore?

A comforting smile.

                    LEVINO
          …That's right honey.

                    JULIA
          And is it true that we're not
          gonna see you so much when you
          come back?

Levino's smile fades a little.

                    LEVINO

          That's also true honey.

Janine stands behind Julia.

                    JULIA
          …I was wondering…

Julia stops.

> JULIA(cont'd)
> …I was wondering if maybe… when
> you come back… if you feel like
> it… and you're not very tired…
> maybe we could go to the park…
> and maybe… you can teach me to
> rollerblade…
> JULIA(cont'd)
> (pause)
> …if you're not too tired…

Levino smiles genuinely for the first time. These
are the moments he lives for.

> LEVINO
> …When I get back Julia, I'll
> teach you how to rollerblade
> and we'll put some more stamps
> in your stamp collection.

> JULIA
> All sorts of stamps?

> LEVINO
> All sorts of stamps.

Levino's cell-phone goes off.

> LEVINO (cont'd)
> Hon, I gotta go… what's my cell
> phone number?

Julia rattles it off with lightning speed.

> JULIA
> 415-335-2687

Levino nods, satisfied. Janine comes to the
screen. A beat as she looks at Levino, expression
heavy with unspoken words. She pulls Julia away.

71. INT. DETENTION CENTER, WASH ROOM - LATER

Levino rubs his hands under a jetting faucet,
lathering his ring finger with soap. Steam rises
across his morbid expression. He twists his ring
off, gritting.
CLINK.

Levino looks down through the steam. His wedding
ring lays beside the drain.

72. INT. BASEMENT - NIGHT

The door opens. Amira enters. Khassem's face
softens. Amira comes in slowly. She moves to
where Hamza is, without making eye contact with
the others. She sits, her back to the room.

Larbi and Khassem stare at her. The silence,
heavy.

                    KHASSEM
          Amira.

                    LARBI
          Leave her alone.

                    KHASSEM
          Amira.

                    LARBI
          Leave her alone!

                    KHASSEM
          Say something Amira.

A beat.

                    AMIRA
          ...I didn't talk.

Suddenly the SOUND OF FOOTSTEPS outside. Hamza
involuntarily jerks forward.

Amira looks into Hamza's eyes. Sees his fear. The
steps come nearer, then fade. Hamza cringes.
Amira looks into Hamza's eyes, concerned.

                    AMIRA
          You won't talk, will you?

Hamza tries to look away.

                    AMIRA
          Answer me.

                    HAMZA
          I don't know. I thought I was
          strong enough but when I saw
          you brought in…
                    (beat)
          I know they hurt you.

                    AMIRA
                    (hard)
          They didn't touch me! No one
          touched me! Nothing happened!

Hamza looks away.

                    AMIRA
          Hamza, they only hurt me if you
          talk.

                    LARBI
          Hamza already talked.

The room crashes — a sudden silence. Then Amira
turns, faces the room, faces Hamza.

                    AMIRA
          What do you mean? When?

                    LARBI
          When they took his prints.
                  (to Hamza)
          You told them you distributed
          guns.

Hamza looks around the room, almost panic-
stricken.

                    HAMZA
          I didn't say anything.

Larbi nods slowly, as if confirming something to
himself.

                    LARBI
                  (quietly)
          It was you.

                    HAMZA
                  (fervent)
          I didn't say anything Larbi.

                    LARBI
          How did they know then?

                    HAMZA
          I don't know.

Hamza's jaw shakes. His eyes fill with tears. He
points suddenly, towards Khassem.

              HAMZA (cont'd)
          Maybe it was him.

Khassem stares hard at Larbi.

                  KHASSEM
          What are you trying to do?

                    LARBI
          I'm saying someone talked,
          that's all.

                    KHASSEM
          And if someone talked, it has
          to be me.

Khassem's eyes mask disgust.

                    KHASSEM (cont'd)
          Don't you realize I'm suffering
          more than any of you?

Hamza laughs through tears suddenly. Bitterly.

                    HAMZA
          You want pity?

Khassem folds his arms.

                    KHASSEM
          Yes. That's right. You could
          allow yourself some pity and
          respect.

Larbi sneers, looks away.

                    HAMZA
          We're going to die and you're
          worse off.

                    AMIRA
          Hamza.

                    HAMZA
                    (explodes)
          You want to stop suffering?!
          I'll do you a favor and end it!
          I'll talk! So you can be one of
          us!

                    KHASSEM
          Go ahead. You don't know how
          much I want you to.

Amira suddenly grabs Hamza by the neck.

                              AMIRA
               Look at me! Don't-betray-him.

                              HAMZA
               Why is he special? Why are we
               dying for him?

                              AMIRA
               Because he gets to carry on the
               fight out there.

                              HAMZA
               So what.

Hamza pulls away from Amira, stands.

                         HAMZA (cont'd)
               I'll still tell them verything.
               You think I have a problem with
               that? You think I'm scared of
               our men? When I look at you…
               just a bunch of maniacs, all I
               can think of is… I'm not scared
               of you anymore.

Hamza stares hard at the others, confident.

                              HAMZA
               I want to live.

An uncertain silence. The room absorbs Hamza's
sudden defiance.

                              LARBI
               They won't let you live, Hamza.
               Even if you talk.

                              HAMZA
                       (motions to Khassem)
               Fine. But at least I'll get to
               see him suffer.

Larbi watches Hamza, measuring him.

                    LARBI
                (to Amira)
        Do you think he'll talk?

Amira shifts her gaze to Hamza. A long beat. She
finally nods.

Larbi rises, goes to Hamza. His eyes look
different, brutal.

                    LARBI
        Hamza, I'm not your judge. At
        your age, I'd probably have
        done the same thing.

Hamza takes a step backward. The confidence
drains from his eyes.

                    HAMZA
        What do you mean?

                    LARBI
        We can't let you talk Hamza.
        They plan on killing you either
        way.

A moment's hesitation. Fear.

                    HAMZA
        Fine, I won't talk.

                    LARBI
                (shakes his head)
        The men upstairs know you're
        the weak point. They'll work on
        you till you talk. I won't let
        that happen.

Khassem takes a cautious step towards Larbi.

                    KHASSEM
                (quietly)
        What are you doing?

                    LARBI
               (turns on Khassem)
          We're on the receiving end of
          every bomb, Khassem. This is
          war. And every time one of us
          talks, we take a hundred steps
          back.

                    KHASSEM
          He won't talk.

                    AMIRA
               (to Khassem)
          Why are you interfering?

                    KHASSEM
          Because he's your brother.

                    AMIRA
          He'll die soon.
               (after a beat)
          He needs to be silenced. The
          method doesn't matter.

Hamza, stunned, stares at Amira, then at Larbi.
He suddenly realizes his dilemma and freezes.

                    HAMZA
          You're not going to…

Larbi doesn't answer.

                    HAMZA (cont'd)
          I won't say anything.

Larbi keeps moving towards Hamza.

                    HAMZA
          I won't talk Larbi.

                    KHASSEM
          Give him a chance.

                     LARBI
          We can't afford to give him a
          chance.

They stare at each other for a split second.
There's an animalistic look to Larbi's stare.
Khassem moves away.

Hamza, panic-stricken, suddenly begins to shout.

                    HAMZA
          I don't want to die here!
          Larbi, I'm only sixteen! Let me
          live! Don't kill me in here!
          Larbi grabs him by the throat.

                     LARBI
                (in Arabic)
          In the name of Allah, the most
          merciful…

                    HAMZA
          Amira!

Hamza tries to fight Larbi off but Larbi is too
strong for him.

Amira turns her head towards the opposite wall.
Khassem stares on, disbelieving.

73. INT. DETENTION CENTER, SURVEILLANCE ROOM

Baker paces, smoking, angry. Pent up rage sends
him back and forth across the room.

Sedgwick throws nervous looks. He turns to the
monitor, freezes.

                   SEDGWICK
          Shit.

Baker stops behind him. And suddenly they're up and running…

74. HALLWAY

…down the hallway…

75. BASEMENT

Hamza slides to the floor, making gasping noises, fighting off Larbi with handcuffed hands. An extended, gut-wrenching struggle as Hamza fights for life, legs writhing and kicking on the basement floor.

Then silence. The room absorbs the horrific act. Larbi stands, catching his breath.

75A. BASEMENT

Baker and Sedgwick burst into the room. A THIRD SOLDIER waits by the door, mortified by what he sees.

Baker approaches Hamza, feels his pulse. He looks around the room, repulsed.

                    BAKER
               (to Sedgwick)
          We need to get authorization to
          separate the prisoners.

76. OUTSIDE BASEMENT, HALLWAY

Baker shuts the detainees' steel door behind him, digesting what he just saw. Sedgwick looks shell-shocked.

                    BAKER
          …What a bunch of animals…

77. BASEMENT

Inside the basement, a morbid silence.

Amira painfully makes her way to Hamza, sits down next to him. She takes his head, rests it on her lap.

Khassem can't take his eyes off the body.

                    KHASSEM
                   (quietly)
        What are you all turning into?

Larbi ignores him. Stands over the body.

Amira looks up, meets Larbi's eyes. They share a moment, a bond, an overwhelming surge of emotions.

Then Amira drops her eyes towards Hamza, who looks young, innocent, fearless… a young man asleep.

                    KHASSEM
        He was sixteen.

                    LARBI
        Is anyone in this country
        really sixteen anymore?

Khassem takes a step back, his expression of concern slowly disappearing. He starts to say something, stops. Then he turns around and withdraws into the shadows, away from the others.

                    KHASSEM
                   (quietly)
        There's a way out. If you want
        to live.

No one responds. Khassem keeps his head down.

                    KHASSEM
          Give them the old target list.
                    (beat)

                  KHASSEM (Cont'd)
          We have a new one. And tell
          them our base is across the
          Nouman hospital, at the
          stationary shop. Where the guns
          are.

Nothing except the SOUND OF FOOTSTEPS outside.

Baker comes back in, followed by FOUR SOLDIERS.
He looks around the room, motions the detainees
to their feet.

He turns to the Soldiers, points to Amira and
Larbi.

                    BAKER
          Put 'em in separate rooms.

Baker motions Khassem out. Khassem hesitates,
finally rises. Proceeds Baker out.

78. EXT. OUTSIDE OF BUILDING - NIGHT

Blindfolded, Khassem is led into a black car.

79. INT. CAR - NIGHT

A street. Desert as far as the eye will go. Car
headlights cut through darkness. Then a sudden
stop. Baker and Delaney in the front, a
soldier in the back.

Delaney reaches towards Khassem, pulls off his
hood. Hands him a white envelope with American
bills.

Khassem blinks, looks out into blackness.

80. EXT. STREET - NIGHT

Outside, a lone figure, Khassem watches the car's
red taillights recede as they move further way
from him… becoming a distant memory, a past life…

A beat. Then he takes a step into desert, into
nothingness. Towards freedom.

81. EXT. SECURITY CHECKPOINT, STREET - DUSK

A road between Hilla and Karbala. A checkpoint
sealed off by 3 MIDDLE EASTERN SECURITY FORCES.
M-16 rifles dangle at their sides.

An approaching car.

The Guards raise their M-16's, motion the car to
stop. The car plows on, ignoring the hand
signals.

One of the GUARDS fires his gun in the air. The
car doesn't slow.

A split second of panic before the Guards
exchange a final glance.

Suddenly, A BLAST OF GUNFIRE from the M-16's.
Shells SLAM into the car's windshield, the front
tires, the hood. A cloud of sand as the car spins
off the road, grinds to a stop.

No movement inside. Two bodies — DRIVER and
PASSENGER — slump over, immobile.

A pause. Then more SHELLS BLAST the car.
The Guards — shaking hands, eyes burning with
fear — keep shooting…

                    REPORTER (V.O)
          …Monday's fatal shooting at the
          checkpoint happened along Route
          9 near Najaf, about 20 miles
          north of the site of Saturday's
          suicide bombing…

82. INT. OFFICE - NIGHT

An office. Stacks of papers, files, computer
disks. A sense of chaos. In the background, the
radio sputters news.

A WOMAN'S voice…

                    REPORTER (V.O)
          The Central Command said
          initial reports from the
          confrontation indicated the
          soldiers followed the rules of
          engagement to protect
          themselves. The statement says,
          "In light of recent terrorist
          attacks, the soldiers exercised
          considerable restraint to avoid
          the unnecessary loss of life…"

Levino hashes out reports.

Delaney reads a letter with a picture of his
fiancée attached. His eyes smile. There is a
glint of overwhelming happiness in his eyes.

Underneath that letter are more letters,
meticulously organized in the order of their
arrivals.

Baker comes in.

                    BAKER
          Sir. Forty-eight prisoners just
          got released.

Delaney looks up from his letter.

>   LEVINO
>   Why'd they get released?

>   BAKER
>   Sir, they had no intelligence
>   value.

Levino stops what he's doing, slowly looks up.

>   LEVINO
>   Who said they had no intel
>   value?

>   BAKER
>   Sir, I got that from the intel
>   people.

>   LEVINO
>   You tell J2 not to release
>   anybody from now on.

>   BAKER
>   The forty-eight had been
>   cleared. All employees from the
>   Ishtar hotel.

>   LEVINO
>   I don't care.

>   BAKER
>   Sir, they were too many. We
>   can't guard and feed all of
>   'em.

>   LEVINO
>   You know just as damn well as I
>   do when they get released, they
>   talk to their friends and all
>   our work, all our planning
>   falls by the wayside.

                         BAKER
               Sir, if I…

                        LEVINO
                  (biting his head off)
               DON'T FUCKING RELEASE ANYBODY
               UNTIL I SAY SO.

A pause. Baker grinds his teeth, pacing the
hallway leading up to the office, in and out, in
and out. It's nerve wracking.

Levino gives him a look. Baker abruptly stops,
leans against the wall, facing the window.

A long moment. Baker looks to Levino, tries to
reconcile.

                         BAKER
               Sir, heard what the military
               analyst said on TV?

Levino ignores him. Baker masks frustration,
pushes on.

                    BAKER (cont'd)
               He said kill 1,000 for every
               hostage killed. No need to
               discriminate either.

This time Levino does look up.

                        LEVINO
               When was this?

                         BAKER
               Three hours ago. You didn't see
               it?

                        LEVINO
               Haven't seen a paper in the
               last three hours. Or TV.

BAKER
You really should see the news,
sir. Keep abreast of things.

Levino says nothing.

BAKER
Delaney, when did the analyst
talk about killin' 1,000 for
every one?

DELANEY
Day before yesterday.

BAKER
Zero tolerance policy.
This is why we should have
hammered them from the
beginning. We were too soft.

LEVINO
No we were not too soft. We
have two dead detainees on our
hands. One of them's a kid for
Christ sake. This whole unit's
going under investigation.

BAKER
Well, shit happens. War is
hell, sir. What the fuck else
are we supposed to do?!

LEVINO
I want you to accept the
situation. And all of us have
to face the reality of a
possible court martial, or
discharge.

                    BAKER
                 (to himself)
         Tell you the truth I don't give
         a good fuck anymore. I'll be
         outside.

Baker storms out. Levino shakes his head, pours
himself a glass of whiskey, eyeing Delaney.

                    LEVINO
         Why aren't you drinking?

                    DELANEY
                 (uncomfortable)
         Can't. I promised my fiancee I
         wouldn't come back to her a
         raging alcoholic.

Levino pours him a glass, holding it out.

                    LEVINO
         Here.

                    DELANEY
         I can't.

                    LEVINO
         It's an order. Drink.
                 (beat)
         Relax.

Delaney takes the drink. Levino CLINKS glasses
with him.

                    LEVINO
         To your fiancee.

                    DELANEY
         ...Sandra.

They sip whiskey.

                    LEVINO
        How's she feel about this?

                    DELANEY
        ...She's scared.

                    LEVINO
        That right?

                    DELANEY
        She thinks I should resign.
        Take up a teaching job or
        something.

Levino pulls a cigarette from his pocket,
lighting up. He takes a long drag, smoke settling
around him.

                    LEVINO
        Not everyone's cut out for
        this. It's a filthy job.

Levino empties his glass.

83. HALLWAY

Levino and Delaney go down the hallway. Baker
abruptly follows.

                    BAKER
        If it were up to me, I'd just
        waste 'em.

                    LEVINO
        It's not up to you.

                    DELANEY
        You do that and you give them
        just what they want. Turn them
        into martyrs. They love death.
        Love the sacrifice.

> BAKER
> So let's give 'em what they
> want.

> LEVINO
> Let's not help them into
> martyrdom. If they talk, we
> spare 'em.

> BAKER
> (shakes his head in disgust)
> We treat 'em like men, we've lost
> control of our interrogation.

> DELANEY
> We don't stand to gain much by
> treating them like dogs.

They stop outside Larbi's cell. Levino motions to
Delaney and Baker to stay behind.

84. INT. ISOLATION CELL

Two Soldiers guard the door step aside. Levino
enters alone. Faces Larbi. Sits on the floor
across from him. Awkward tension hangs over the
room.

Levino searches Larbi's expression. Larbi's face
falls stone-faced, glazed with sweat.

> LEVINO
> How long has it been since
> you've had any sleep?

A silence. Finally…

> LARBI
> A long time.

> LEVINO
> Longer I've been here, the
> harder it is to sleep.

Outside - the distant SNAPPING of MACHINE
GUNFIRE.

> LEVINO
> Ever get used to that noise?

Larbi nods. Slowly. Reluctantly.

> LARBI
> It's not the noise. It's the
> things you see that never go
> away.

> LEVINO
> I've seen things too. And they
> never go away. You're right
> about that.

Their eyes connect and it's two men now, just
talking.

> LEVINO
> Larbi… What did you do to the
> boy?

No answer.

> LEVINO (cont'd)
> He was gonna talk and you
> stopped him.

> LARBI
> None of us wanted to talk.

> LEVINO
> Why'd you do it?

Nothing.

> LEVINO
> I respect your fight. It
> doesn't look like it, but I do.

Larbi looks away, stoic.

                    LEVINO
          If you give me the information
          I need, I'll spare your lives.

Larbi leans against the wall, eyeing Levino. He
doesn't answer.

Levino finally stands.

                    LARBI
          If we agree, what proof have we
          got that you'll let us live?

                    LEVINO
                  (cautious)
          You have my word.

The two men look at each other.

                    LARBI
          Then what? What will you do
          with us?

                    LEVINO
          Hand you over to your
          government.

Larbi stares straight into Levino's eyes. Nods
finally.

                    LARBI
          Okay. But she knows some of the
          names on the target list. Let
          me talk to her.

No answer.

                    LARBI (cont'd)
          I think I can persuade her.

Levino looks deep into Larbi's eyes. Then he goes to the door, opens it.

                    LEVINO
                (to the Soldiers)
          Bring the girl in.

The Soldiers leave.

                    LEVINO
                (to Larbi)
          One minute.

Levino closes the door behind him.

85. ISOLATION CELL - SAME

A silence as Larbi stares at the floor. The steel door scrapes open.

Amira is led in. She sits across from him, stares into his eyes. For a long time, they say nothing.

                    AMIRA
          You've decided to talk?

A silence. Long.

                    LARBI
                (quietly)
          We're dying for nothing.

Amira shakes her head, dismissive.

                    LARBI (cont'd)
          If I let myself be killed now
          when I can fight this war and
          win, then nothing could be more
          stupid than my death.

Amira leans her head back, stares at the ceiling. She looks almost defeated.

                    AMIRA
          They destroyed me Larbi.

                    LARBI
          Tomorrow a bomb could end them.
          They're not doing any better
          than us.

Amira merely shakes her head.

86. EXT. STREET - FLASHBACK

Kadhimiya. A middle-class neighborhood. A 9-year old GIRL rides her bicycle along a tree-lined street, cycling through puddles, lifting her head to let rain spray her face...

87. INT. HALLWAY - NIGHT

The image quietly fades. Tears come to Amira's eyes. She stares at the pock-marked ceiling for a long time.

                    AMIRA
          Maybe you're right.

They look into each other's eyes. Larbi smiles gently.

                    AMIRA
          Are we doing the right thing?

                    LARBI
          Of course. Everyone has the
          right to live.

More tears come. Larbi turns to the Soldiers.

                    LARBI
          Tell them we're ready to talk.

One of the Soldiers opens the door. Larbi slowly exhales. Levino, Delaney, and Baker move in.

                    LARBI
                    (calm)
        In Aadhamiya, across the Nouman
        hospital, there's a stationary
        shop. In the back, that's the
        base.

Pause.

                    LEVINO
        The names on the target list?

                    LARBI
        I'll write them down.

Delaney hands Larbi a piece of paper and a pen.
Larbi writes slowly, methodically. When he's
done, he hands the paper to Levino.

                    LEVINO
        Take them out.

The Soldiers take Amira and Larbi out.

88. INT. INTERROGATION ROOM

Delaney and Levino go to the table, make their
final notes in the files.

                    DELANEY
        You believe them?

                    LEVINO
        The story matches Khassem's.

Levino sits at his desk, jotting down the last
details of his report. He sets his pens down,
leaning back in his chair.

                    LEVINO
                    (to Baker)
        Make sure they get turned over
        to their government.

Baker nods, leaving.

89. INT. INTERROGATOR'S OFFICE

Levino empties his personals from his desk. He
glances at a yellow post-it message on his desk,
slumps involuntarily. He takes his cell phone,
dials.

> LEVINO
> (into phone)
> Colonel. You there?

> COLONEL BILL LARSON (V.O)
> No, you're talking to a
> recording. What the hell is it?

Levino eyes the post-it message.

> LEVINO
> (into phone)
> You said to call. I'm call…

> COLONEL BILL LARSON (V.O)
> (cutting him off)
> How are you?

> LEVINO
> Well, I'm getting a start on
> packing my shit.

> COLONEL BILL LARSON (V.O)
> Don't bother. There's not going
> to be an investigation.

Levino, shocked into silence.

> COLONEL BILL LARSON (V.O)
> Nobody wants to draw any more
> negative attention to this
> whole damn mess. Besides you
> got the target list. Good job.

                    LEVINO
          Thanks.

Larson hangs up. Levino sets his phone down. He
shakes his last cigarette in his hand, lighting
his Zippo. No spark. He tosses the Zippo aside,
searching for a match.

90. EXT. OUTSIDE OF BUILDING - NIGHT

Larbi and Amira are led into a black SUV.

91. INT. CAR - NIGHT

A stretch of darkness. A lone SUV on the road.
Two Middle Eastern Police in the front of the
SUV. Sedgwick in the back.

The SUV suddenly pulls over. The Police motion
Larbi and Amira out.

92. EXT. STREET - NIGHT
Outside, Amira and Larbi have their hoods and
handcuffs removed.

One of the Policemen shoves them forward.

                    POLICEMAN
                 (in Arabic)
          Go.

Larbi and Amira hesitate, exchange a look.
Then slowly, they move forward, their back to the
Policemen.

Sedgwick hangs back, at the back passenger door.
One of the Policeman slowly lifts his 9mm.
SUDDENLY A SHARP GUNSHOT. Larbi goes down.
ANOTHER SHARP GUNSHOT. Amira's body follows.

                    SEDGWICK
                (under his breath)
          Fuck!

93. INT. DETENTION CENTER, HALLWAY

Sedgwick charges down the hallway, not going fast enough…

94. INT. INTERROGATION ROOM

He flings the door open, heads straight for Levino. He leans in, speaking quietly. Midway through Sedgwick's speech, Levino's head snaps up, towards Baker. The shock on his face is evident.

                    LEVINO
          Jesus.

Baker sees the exchange, gets it. His face goes defiant.

                    BAKER
          Zero tolerance policy. They
          live, their insurgent movement
          gets stronger. They disappear,
          problem solved.

LEVINO SUDDENLY GOES FOR BAKER, CRASHING HIS FIST INTO BAKER'S FACE, SLAMMING HIM TO THE FLOOR. BAKER SHAKES LEVINO OFF. LEVINO LUNGES FOR HIM AGAIN, PUNCHING.

Delaney comes at both men, pulls them apart. The door opens. Nelson on the other side. He stares at the mayhem, stunned.

Then he speaks, suddenly. Nervously. Robotically.

                    NELSON
                 (to Levino)
          …Sir, a transport just arrived
          with four new prisoners.

The room — tense. Levino, unable to speak. Delaney takes charge.

                    DELANEY
        What do we have on them?

                    NELSON
        Widmark's beheading.

Nelson nervously brings a set of files to the
table. Baker stands against the wall, calming
down.

Delaney goes to the table, looks through the
file, stops on one of the pictures.

                    DELANEY
            Bring him in.

Nelson halts at the door, still a little
disconcerted. Then he leaves.

Levino moves to the window, staring down ten
flights, at FOUR NEW HOODED DETAINEES being led
into the building.

Another round. Another batch. More
interrogations. It never ends.

                              CUT TO BLACK

*The screenplay was inspired by the writings of Jean-Paul Sartre.

PRE-PRODUCTION EMAILS

Cetywa Powell

To Waleed, Reyad
10/28/05 at 12:50 AM

Met with Mali Finn. I will get a cover letter tomorrow to her, first thing, and immediately after, she will be fedexing (Friday morning) the script to Willem Dafoe and Woody Harrelson (Baker) for a Saturday delivery.

Also, Waleed... I sent the Tribeca letter fedex. You should receive it Friday morning.

Talk soon,
Cetywa

Cetywa Powell

To Waleed, Reyad
12/09/05 at 1:17 PM

Mali Finn just called me. She said both agents' ears perked up when the offer was raised. Frank (Willem Dafoe's manager) will get the script to him immediately. Woody Harrelson's play in London has been extended to march 24th. She asked if that was okay. I said, at least get him to read it and see if he's interested. If not, then his extension won't matter. If he is, then the three of us can talk about what to do next.

So...

That's the latest.

And she said December 19th is an absolute answer from them... Definite yes or definite no. Right?

Cetywa Powell

To Nicky
11/01/05 at 9:44 AM

Hey Nicky,

Mali Finn called me yesterday. She said Willem Dafoe
will be shooting a low-budget film in NY Jan through
mid-February but will be available in March (it must
be the film you were talking about). Mali also said
that Woody Harrelson will be doing a play in London in
January and February. I talked to both Waleed and
Reyad yesterday. We agree that we should shoot early
March to keep both actors (assuming they're both
interested).

Another thing she said was that $65,000 is the minimum
actors should be paid in order to get free rehearsal
(for a 500K budget). So we're going to offer both
actors that amount.

That's the latest...

Cetywa Powell

To Aki Avni
12/19/05 at 12:08 PM

Aki,

Mali Finn just called. Woody Harrelson likes the script. Wow! The only thing is that he wants to play Levino instead of Baker (which is fine with me). The other thing is that there are two other projects that he wants to do so he'd like to know how flexible we are with our shooting schedule.

We will be ironing out the details in the next few days. Will keep you updated.

Cetywa

Cetywa Powell

To Aki Avni
01/07/06 at 12:58 AM

Hey Aki,

Thank you for your support and your involvement. It means a lot to me.

Okay... now for the latest. I spoke with Woody Harrelson's assistant today. I "officially" offered the role of Levino to him. She said he's definitely interested. There are a lot of things to iron out, possible problems. His schedule is packed solid and the possible earliest he can squeeze us in for the shoot is the 2 last weeks of May. Which means (maybe) 4 weeks rehearsal in April. 4 weeks shoot for you in May (and the last 2 weeks Woody Harrelson comes on). The film may be a five week shoot but the last week we don't need him or you.

Woody's schedule: he's in a play till March 24th. Then he's booked a film from March 27th to mid-May. Hopefully, we're next. Now, he hasn't signed any contract for the film shooting March 27th, so his assistant, (Tracy Harshman) will fill me in on that when it happens.

The possible problems are a couple:

1) He won't be leaving London because the film after his play will be shot in London. Also, his wife is pregnant and is expecting a baby end of May/early June. So she can't travel which means he doesn't want to travel. That means (possibly), if we shoot with him late May, we may have to shoot those scenes in London. More money, more headache... we'll see. If we have to do it, we have to do it.

2) Secondly, we may not get rehearsal time with him.
We can rehearse the rest of the cast and then he'll
come on set and shoot (which doesn't make me happy as
a director), but again, if we have to make it work, we
have to make it work.

I'll be working out the details with Tracy in the next
two weeks and trying hard to make it work for us and
for him.

So... we'll see.

It's one in the morning and I'm tired!

Talk soon.

C

Cetywa Powell

To Zuaiter, Waleed
01/09/06 at 2:55 PM

The press at INDIEWIRE wants to do an interview with
me about 'Dirty Hands'. We haven't made the film so I
have no clue what to say. They contacted Tribeca who
then forwarded the email to me.

That's the latest. I think it's pretty definite we'll
have Woody Harrelson the last week or 2 weeks of May.
It may be the last week of May and the first week of
June or the last 2 weeks of May. Theoretically, yes.
Legally no. Because the film he's shooting before
ours will not give an end date (and legally, they
don't have to in case of pick ups, etc). So
theoretically we can say May 21st to June 4th but
that's only if all goes perfectly on the previous
shoot. So our shoot days (give or take a week or so)
is dependent on their wrap date and I'm not sure we
can do much about that.

Let's have a conference call. Tomorrow at 10:30a.m?
I want to call Tracy afterwards.

Cetywa Powell

To Waleed, Reyad
01/12/06 at 11:12 AM

Just so you know guys, Jeremy Plager at CAA (Woody's
agent) is not at all supportive of us doing this film
with Woody. So we're fighting him to keep Woody.
He's going to make it difficult for us.

Just so you know.

Cetywa Powell

To Waleed, Reyad
01/17/06 at 1:10 PM

I've heard back from Tracy, which is good. The two
emails I sent were:
1) a revised script to Woody Harrelson
and
2) If we could get Woody's input on casting Baker.

I wanted her to respond because it meant he's still
interested and still wants to do this movie (just a
psychological peace of mind, if you know what I mean).

Go ahead and email the draft letter tomorrow morning.
I told Tracy that I am giving both you and Reyad her
email address (I don't think Fred should be CC'ed on
it because I don't know how many people she wants
having her email address... what do you think?) It
should just be the three of us for now (you, me,
Reyad).

Cetywa Powell

To Tracy
02/08/06 at 1:50 PM

Hey Tracy,

Just so you know, we have an American Interrogator as an advisor for the actors and for the movie. So if Woody Harrelson needs to ask any questions in the future, let me know and I will put him in touch with the American Interrogator (he served in Afghanistan and supervised all military interrogations there).

Thanks,
Cetywa

Cetywa Powell

To Nicky
02/27/06 at 9:40 AM

Here's what's happening.

Our first dates are in May (18 days). We won't be
shooting in London anymore because scheduling a shoot
around a pregnancy proved too dangerous and unstable
for us. So we asked when Woody was available after
that...

It will be 18 days in May and then the last two weeks
of August (for Woody Harrelson's scenes). But they
will take place in the U.S. So the entire shoot will
be in Los Angeles now (except for the Dubai stuff).

I have not talked about the money going in the bank...
the reaon is that Jeremy Plager (Woody's agent) is
dead set against Woody doing this movie and is
stalling on the contract. It's hard to get investors
to put money in the bank without a letter from Woody.
That's why I'm going to London. To talk with Woody
and ask for a letter from him becasue Jeremy is doing
anything he can to make sure Woody is not in this
film.

But dates are: May and August (and in between we will
do exteriors in Dubai/Turkey as well as start the
editing so that we can finish the editing by September
in time for Sundance). It will be hectic but we're
pushing for it to happen.

Another friend is also looking for a place for me in
London... so we'll see.

Cetywa Powell

To Waleed, Reyad
02/25/06 at 12:30 AM

Jeremy Plager emailed me. I am not forwarding his
email but quoting a little of what he said here... my
concern here is that it looks like they may change
their mind due to overexposure? Because he's doing
too many films and ours would be the one to cut? It
worries me.

Jeremy's words:
"My reservations for Woody lie solely in his time. An
actor can only do a certain number of films in any
given year or he becomes over exposed. Woody is
already set to do 2 films by August and
we need to sort out a 3rd film which will go sometime
in the fall. I have reservations about him doing DIRTY
HANDS at this time for that reason. I hope this clears
up any nervousness you may have about my stance. Your
script is very provocative and could be a very
interesting film."

Cetywa Powell

To Waleed, Reyad
04/21/06 at 10:14 AM

Let's have a conference call when both of you are available. I'm available all day.

--- "Zuaiter, Waleed" wrote:

> Hey guys,
>
> As we feared and anticipated, we officially got a
> pass from Tracy
> regarding Woody Harrelson. I got a call from her
> yesterday right before
> my show and I got out late so couldn't call or
> write.
>
> Basically, he hasn't even seen the reel (sorry
> Cetywa), he's been so
> busy with filming, and he won't be able to get back
> with an answer by
> today. Basically, if we didn't put a time
> constraint on an
> answer, my feeling is that he'll continue to string
> us along hoping that
> he'll commit.
>
> Well according to Tracy, "as of now we can take this
> as an official no."
> I specifically asked her that we need to look for
> another actor to fill
> the role, and that in order to do that we need to
> get the official no,
> and that's when she said it. She did say that if he
> changes his mind
> after seeing the reel and considering the other
> option with the DP and

> thinks about it, she'll call us back and see where
> we are with
> recasting, and if we already have someone else
> they'll understand that
> they missed out. I don't think they'll call back.
> We can't wait any
> longer. They have wasted 4 months of our time
> thinking we have him, we
> need to make up this lost time and regroup to
> stategize going forward.
>
> If we can talk this afternoon and have a conference
> call, that would be
> great. I'm available pretty much until 4:00pm NYC
> time.
>
> We need to plan to have a call (the three of us)
> with Mali Finn on
> Monday.
>
> Waleed
>

*The production fell apart soon after Woody Harrelson's pass on the project.

PRISON STORY

1. INT. PRISON, MESS HALL — DAY

JACK, standard prison uniform, unshaven, watchful eyes. A former research scientist and respectable looking man if it weren't for the uniform. He eats hard spaghetti. Typical prison food.

ART sidles over to him. Cocky, a smooth talker, clean cut, black hair that's been slicked back. Piercing eyes.

                    ART
          Mind if I join you?

Jack keeps his eyes on his food. Art smiles. Slowly.

                    ART (Cont'd)
          Did you do it?

                    JACK
               (looking up)
          Do what?

                    ART
          What you're in for.

Jack's eyes go cold. He looks across at Art.

                    JACK
          How'd you end up here?

                    ART
White collar stuff. Embezzlement. Money, jewelry, drugs.

                    JACK
          Drugs isn't a white collar
          crime.

                    ART
          White drugs.

Jack stares at Art, unimpressed. Art stares back, a sly grin plastered on his face.

                    ART (Cont'd)
          I heard you were a real hot
          research scientist.

                    JACK
          What do you want?

Art looks at Jack surprised.

                    ART
          Just making conversation.

                    JACK
          No you're not, you're bothering
          me.

Art's face breaks into another grin.

                    ART
          I like you.

He studies Jack, nodding. After a while—

                    ART (cont'd)
          I think you could help me
          escape.

Jack says nothing. A glass shatters. Heads turn. Art turns back to Jack. Jack keeps his eyes focused on the fight taking place a few tables up.

                    ART
          I mean the two of us.

                    JACK
          We're in the middle of a
          desert. You can't do it.

The noise dies down. One of the prisoners, a STOCKY MAN, gets dragged out by two security guards.

                    ART
          I've planned this for months.
          Everything's detailed. Every
          pitfall's been thought out.

Jack picks up his tray, uninterested. Art shoves a tightly folded piece of paper towards him.

                    ART (Cont'd)
          Here's the plan
               (pauses, watches Jack)
          Think about it.

Jack starts walking. Art pulls him back.

                    ART
          I trust you with that.

They lock eyes for a split second. Jack takes the paper and walks away.

2. INT. PRISON CELL — NIGHT

Jack looks over the plan with a flashlight. The plan is detailed, with maps and directions. He reads it thoroughly, then folds the paper, tucks it into his pants, and goes to sleep.

3. INT. MESS HALL — DAY

Jack waits in the food line. Art comes up to him.

                    ART
          So?

                    JACK
          (slips the paper into Art's pocket)
          I want no part of it.

                    ART
                (whispering)
        We've got others helping out!

                    JACK
        No.

Jack gets his serving and moves forward to a
table. Art remains behind, fuming silently.

4. EXT. PRISON GROUNDS — NIGHT

Art emerges from the sewer pipe. He crawls in the
shadows, sees a guard, ducks, and runs.

5. EXT. DESERT — DAY

An exhausted Art stumbles in sand. Falls. He gets
back on his feet and stumbles forward.

6. EXT. DESERT—NIGHT

Art walks forward slowly, parched lips, swollen
eyes. An approaching Land Rover blinds him. He
crouches. The Land Rover stops.

Two PRISON GUARDS emerge. They poke their rifles
into Art's ribs. Art tries to run, can't. He
throws his hands in the air, a defeated man.

7. INT. PRISON, MESS HALL — DAY

Metal gates CLANG shut. The camera pulls back to
see a black and blue Art eating painfully. He
swallows and grimaces.

Jack sits across from him.

                    JACK
        Didn't make it out, huh?
            (Art ignores him)
        I heard they gave you solitary
        for six months.

Jack studies him.

                    JACK (Cont'd)
          Sorry you didn't get out.

Art pushes his food away. The swollen right side
of his face twitches.

                    ART
          I gave myself in.

                    JACK
          I'm not surprised. I tried it
          once and went through the same
          thing.

Art snaps awake. His black eyes bulge.

                    ART
          You what?! Why didn't you tell
          me before I made my break?

Jack chews slowly, suppressing a smile.

                    JACK
          In my field of research, we
          never announce negative
          results.

Art lunges for him. Jack gets thrown on the
floor. Food flies in all directions. The two go
at it, punching, kicking. Inmates surround them,
egging them on. A PRISON GUARD breaks it apart.

                    PRISON GUARD
               (turns to Art)
          You're going back to solitary.

INT. PRISON CELL, SOLITARY CONFINEMENT—DAY

Art gets dragged to a single, dark cell. The
GUARD locks a heavy metal door, walks away.

The sound of his footsteps recede in the distance.

CUT TO BLACK

ONLY FIRECRACKERS

FADE IN ON:

A black screen. The sound of heavy traffic noise.
Then a voice—

> OSCAR (V.O)
> I've been thinking about my
> father and the last time I saw
> him…

1. INT. MCDONALDS — NIGHT

Under harsh fluorescent lights, OSCAR STREATY
(32) picks at some fries.

Age is beginning to show on Oscar's face: creases
of life, hardship, worry. His sad eyes, however,
seem to have found a measure of peace.

> OSCAR (V.O)
> It was San Francisco. In the
> summer. Five years ago. And it
> was my oldest brother's
> wedding. We were all scared
> because it was the first time
> in twelve years that the whole
> family had gotten together…

As Oscar stands, we see a black suitcase next to
him.

> OSCAR (V.O)
> We never wanted to be together.
> There were just too many bad
> memories. But this time, we
> were older and maybe had
> figured out how to put some
> stuff behind us.

2. EXT. STREET — NIGHT

At a crosswalk, the light turns green and Oscar
drags his suitcase across the tarmac.

OSCAR (V.O)
But I remember I was sitting in
my sister's living room, trying
not to look nervous. And we
were all talking, nobody really
saying anything important. We
were waiting for the doorbell
to ring.
(a beat)
We were waiting for my father.

3. INT. SUBWAY STATION — LATER

Going down the escalator subway, Oscar looks at
blinking eyes strobing on a wall.

OSCAR (V.O)
And when the doorbell rang,
there was this silence. And I
remember when my sister got the
door and we saw my father
standing there. It was like
this old man I didn't
recognize. And just looking at
him, I realized what alcohol
had done to him, how it had
destroyed his body, and had
gotten his ankles swollen and
his hands shaking and his eyes
yellow…

Inside the station, Oscar punches in a "one-way"
fare, slides in correct change and waits for his
paper ticket to pop out of the machine.

And as Oscar slowly takes his luggage down to the
subway platform, his face softens.

OSCAR (V.O)
He looked so weak. And tired.

4. INT. SUBWAY PLATFORM — NIGHT

Dim lights from the subway tunnel bright as the
red subway line going downtown pulls into the
station. There's a flurry of activity and
PASSENGERS board the train.

                    OSCAR (V.O)
          Later, my mother told us that
          he was vomiting all the time.
          That he just stayed in his room
          all day and watched TV. That he
          was wearing diapers because all
          the drinking over the years had
          destroyed his bladder. And he
          was wearing dentures because
          the drinking and vomiting had
          rotted his teeth.

5. INT. TRAIN — DAY

A crowded subway car. Bored PASSENGERS stare out
of dirt-stained windows.

                    OSCAR (V.O)
          At the time, I just listened
          because I didn't know what to
          say.

Oscar finds a window seat. And as his body
relaxes into the seat, a deep sadness comes over
him.

                    OSCAR (V.O)
          But later, when I was alone, I
          cried. Remembering what he said
          to me once. He said, "I know
          they've been good times, but I
          can't remember any."

The conductor's muted voice comes over the
loudspeaker as the train pulls to a stop.

And Oscar, looking through the window, rushes for the door and out to the platform.

6. EXT. SUBWAY PLATFORM — THE SAME TIME

> OSCAR (V.O)
> After my brother's wedding, I got real worried because I kept expecting a phone call maybe in the middle of the night, saying my father was vomiting blood, saying he had choked on his own vomit.

After a beat.

> OSCAR (V.O)
> But when the call came, it was different. It was my brother and he said, "I don't know how to say this... I just got home and found him at the table with his head back." The paramedics came, said they found his body still warm, said they found food in his throat and they weren't sure if he had a heart attack or if he had choked to death.

Oscar, under a lamp, stares down at the tracks.

As another train comes, Oscar hauls his suitcase into the subway car and stands, facing the window.

7. INT. SUBWAY CAR — NIGHT

For the first time Oscar seems aware of his surroundings. He takes the Passengers in... the GIRL with the chipped black nail polish next to him, the WOMAN with roses, the pot-bellied OLD MAN asleep in his seat...

Finally his gaze goes back to the window and to the dark streets beyond.

                    OSCAR (V.O)
          So that's how I got the news.

8.EXT. STREET - NIGHT

With the subway ride over, Oscar comes down an escalator, towards a street, towards a bus stop.

There's a bus already waiting, and the BUS DRIVER is motioning for Oscar to hurry up…

                    OSCAR (V.O)
          Now I'm on my way to the
          airport, back to New York, and
          I'm thinking about my father
          and about the things he told
          me. Like the story about the
          noises that would keep him up
          at night when he was a kid and
          how he used to think they were
          gunshots… and he'd laugh and
          say, "…it was only
          firecrackers…"

9. INT. BUS — NIGHT

As the bus moves forward, wider streets converge into one direction: the airport.

Green DEPARTURE and ARRIVAL signs finally come into focus.

                    OSCAR (V.O)
          I'm thinking about my last days
          in New York, at La Guardia
          airport when my father paid
          five dollars for beer and my
          mother ate bad Chinese food.

                    OSCAR (V.O)
          And I remember I couldn't wait
          to leave… and I kept saying
          that I wouldn't come back.

The bus comes to a stop outside *Continental
Airlines.* With the rest of the passengers, Oscar
heads into the airport.

10. INT. AIRPORT — NIGHT

Inside, as the glass doors open, Oscar looks up
at the departure schedule, as electronic signs
unfold.

He finally comes across his own flight: DEPARTURE
- LA TO NEW YORK - CONTINENTAL AIRLINES -
10:52pm.

                    OSCAR (V.O)
          And what I'm wondering is,
          would I have said more to my
          father or hugged him longer if
          I had known that years later my
          father would bring me back
          home…

Oscar goes through the gates, a silent figure
diminishing in size.

                    OSCAR (V.O)
          His death, anyway.

11. OUTSIDE THE AIRPORT — NIGHT

Planes line up on the runway. The air controllers
wave air traffic. And in the sky, 747s become
moving lights.

As we slowly——

                                   FADE TO BLACK

ABOUT CETYWA POWELL

Cetywa Powell is a filmmaker and a photographer.

www.ingramcontent.com/pod-product-compliance
Lightning Source LLC
Chambersburg PA
CBHW070338130626
46556CB00007B/2921